BREAKDOWN

BUDGE WILSON

Cover by Laura Fernandez

Scholastic-TAB Publications Ltd.

Scholastic-TAB Publications Ltd.
123 Newkirk Road, Richmond Hill, Ontario, Canada L4C 3G5

Scholastic Inc.
730 Broadway, New York, NY 10003, USA

Ashton Scholastic Limited
165 Marua Road, Panmure, PO Box 12328, Auckland 6, New
Zealand

Ashton Scholastic Pty Limited
PO Box 579, Gosford, NSW 2250, Australia

Scholastic Publications Ltd.
Holly Walk, Leamington Spa, Warwickshire CV32 4LS,
England

Canadian Cataloguing in Publication Data
Wilson, Budge.
    Breakdown

ISBN 0-590-71843-6

I. Title.

PS8595.I47B73 1988   jC813'.54   C87-095207-2
PZ7.W54Br 1988

8 7 6 5 4 3 2   Printed in Canada   0 1 2 3 4/9
Manufactured by Webcom Limited

Chapter 1

The Collicuts' house stood halfway down the block. Like most Halifax houses, it was made of fine, strong wood, but the white paint was grey with age and one of the front steps was in need of repair. It was an old house, with gingerbread carving around the eaves and above the veranda. There was a large bay window at the front. If you stood on tiptoe at that window and looked east, you could see a little slice of Halifax Harbour behind the grain elevators. The house was close to the sidewalk, with almost no front lawn, and the narrow alleyway was just wide enough for Mr. Collicut's car and a cinder footpath.

Although it was only four o'clock on a Wednesday afternoon, his car was parked there now.

Katie Collicut looked out the kitchen window and sighed. Rain was streaming down the pane, and she could hear the klink-plink of heavy drops hitting the drain under the rain spout. She was feeling gloomy enough as it was without bad weather, too. On her way over to the sink, she sighed again, and then started to fill the dishpan with hot soapy water. Her week to do the dishes.

Another reason to feel sorry for herself. She began dumping cutlery into the pan, taking pleasure in the crash it made as it fell in.

"For Pete's sake!" yelled her father from the TV room. "Do you have to sound like a confounded bomb when you're doing the dishes?" She could hear him slam down his newspaper.

Katie clenched her teeth and shut her eyes. She wanted to yell something back, something like: Why are you allowed to bang around, but no one else is? Why are you so unfair? And so *cranky* all the time?

She unclenched her teeth and whispered the words savagely, rehearsing them in case she ever had the courage to say them out loud. Rehearsing, rehearsing. She took a deep breath and let it out slowly.

Seems to me I've been doing this all my life, she mused. I just wish I could come home from school or from my music lesson or from out talking to Julie, and find a peaceful house for a change. Nobody being mad. No one pushing us around.

She opened her eyes. Her reflection in the mirror above the sink stared back at her. Dark brown eyes in a thirteen-year-old face; pale sandy hair — straight and sleek — falling to her shoulders. She was frowning, and she stuck out her tongue at her own cross face. My eyes are okay, she thought, but I don't know about the rest of me. Sure would like to have curly hair. And not be so thin. To have some *shape*, like Helena Donnely. And to have Olaf Hensen take me to the grade nine graduation dance — nine whole months away. And to win the cup in the Music Festival.

The Music Festival. Katie let her hands dangle in the water and closed her eyes, the better to picture herself in the concert hall. There she was, finishing her Chopin piece, the four dramatic chords at the end filling the hall with sound. She would pause, she thought, before rising from the piano bench. Then, in the midst of a tense silence, she would stand up, head bent, suitably humble, and walk to the front of the stage.

The applause would be deafening, booming and clattering, thunder and rain together. Even the adjudicators would stop writing in order to clap — rising from their seats as they did so. A standing ovation. She imagined herself bowing slowly, then bowing again. Blowing a kiss to her audience, she would leave the stage, her arms full of roses.

Katie stared out the window and smiled, no longer seeing the wet world in front of her. Her whole life was going to be like that dream, she just knew it. The high that music gave her would be followed by the high of admiration and applause. Forever and ever.

"Katie!" It was her father's voice, and she snapped out of her fantasy. "Your mother's due home from the doctor with the twins any minute. She's going to need that sink for getting the vegetables ready. Get moving! You're so damn slow!"

"Mom won't mind," argued Katie. "She says just so's I get them done, she doesn't care when."

"Well, *I* care!" Her father appeared at the doorway, rubbing his temples. "It's a stupid and inefficient way to work." He paused. "Katie, where does your mother keep the aspirin? I've got one heck of a headache, and once those twins are in the door, it'll be a noise factory in here."

Katie reached above the sink and took a small flat tin out of a box beside the baking supplies. "Here," she said, handing it to him. "Take two," she added, an edge to her voice. "How come you're home from work so early?"

He didn't answer. He poured himself a glass of water instead and, taking the aspirin, left the kitchen.

"How come you're home from work so early?" she repeated, this time calling out the question so that he could hear her from his seat in the TV room.

"I *hear* you, Katie! For heaven's sake, I'm not deaf! You don't have to *yell!*" She heard the click of the TV switch, and then the air was filled with blaring sound. Click and click again. Rock music. A news commentary, cut off in mid-sentence: *An earthquake in Mexico resulted in* . . . ; the cheers of fans watching a football game; the confessions of a soap opera heroine: *George. I don't know how*

4

to tell you this, but yesterday . . . Click. Snap. The TV was off.

The back door burst open. It was Daniel. Katie felt relief. Nice, she thought, to have someone in the house who might be a little bit friendly. Daniel flew in, wet clothes and all, yelling, "Dad! *Dad!*" and then asked eagerly, "He's home early, isn't he?"

"Oh, yes," said Katie, rolling her eyes to the ceiling. "He's home all right."

"Hey, *Dad!*" shouted Daniel.

Their father appeared at the kitchen door again, his hand across his forehead.

"Can't anyone just *speak* in this house?" he asked wearily. "You can't believe how your voices actually hit my eardrums. What's the matter, Daniel?"

"Nothing's the matter, Dad. Everything's great. Dad?"

"What?"

"I made the track team. I got chosen today. There was a list up on the bulletin board at recess."

Mr. Collicut's hand came down from his forehead, and his eyes shone.

"Hey, kid! That's really something! I was a great athlete myself until I broke both kneecaps in that car accident. When I was nineteen."

Why are you *always* talking about that car accident, thought Katie. Could you maybe just listen to *Daniel* for a minute?

"Did you make it in all categories?" asked their father.

Daniel lost some of his steam and his eyes looked troubled. "No, Dad," he said. "Just the running."

"How come that's all?" asked Mr. Collicut, frowning. "No broad jump? Hurdles? You've lost your chance to be the all-round winner."

"I thought you'd be pleased," said Daniel, his face bleak. "I ran all the way home to tell you."

"Oh sure, son, sure. I'm pleased. It's just that if you want to be a great athlete, you have to try to be a winner in every single area." He turned around and headed back to the TV room, rubbing his temples again. As he left the kitchen, the kids could hear him muttering, "Otherwise you get left behind."

Katie looked at Daniel. He was biting his nails and the tic in his left eye was going flick-flick.

"I think it's great!" she said. "I never made it even to the *tryouts* for the track team. You know me. I've got two left feet, and I fall over both of them. The only parts of my body that know what to do with themselves are my fingers."

He grinned at her. "Thanks," he said. Then, "I'm gonna practise so hard. If I win a ribbon or something, maybe he'll be proud." He ran his fingers through his bushy brown hair and sighed.

"Lookit, Dan. He's probably proud right now. He's just got a headache or something."

Daniel sat down on a kitchen chair and reached for the cookie tin. "Listen, Katie." He spoke very quietly. "I'm only eleven, so I don't remember everything so good. But was he always like this? Was there ever a time when . . . "

"Well," Katie said as she mopped the dishes and rinsed them. "Yeah. There was. I seem to remember that way back — I'm not sure when — he was different. Not so long ago, really. It just seems long. He was always, well, *pushy* and kind of critical. He always wanted to win everything and be best. Like even at Crazy Eights. But he used to be lotsa fun too, and was all the time showing us he loved us. Hugs and all that stuff." She frowned as she stacked the dishes in the cupboard.

The back door opened again and the twins exploded into the kitchen. Six-year-old boys with identical shaggy blond hair, fair skin and vivid blue eyes. They also each had rashes on their faces and over every visible part of their bodies. They were pinching one another as they entered, squealing with laughter.

"Better put a lid on it, kids," warned Katie, hanging up the dishtowel, then wiping off the counter. "The general's on the warpath against noise today."

Then their mother was in the kitchen too, dumping bags of groceries on the table before sinking into a chair, head back against the wall.

"You okay, Mom?" asked Katie. Usually her

7

mother was forever and ever cheerful, always ready with a joke or a laugh. Then Katie yelled at Daniel, who was escaping upstairs, "Hey, kid! It's your week to set the table. C'mon. I've gotta practise an hour before supper." She looked at her mother again. "You okay?" she repeated.

"Tired," mumbled her mother. "But fine."

The twins had disappeared outside to play in the rain, and Daniel was struggling to get the big tablecloth onto the dining room table.

"How'd it go at the doctor's?" asked Katie, handing her mother the cookie jar. Mrs. Collicut took a cookie and held it in her hand absentmindedly. She sighed.

"Oh, okay, I guess," she said, laying down the cookie and making marks in the oilcloth with her fingernail. "It's just that I'd like a miracle." She chuckled. "I'd like to see a blinding flash of light in the sky over Citadel Hill, followed maybe by the sound of violins, and then open my eyes and find the twins' rashes gone.

"I'd almost be satisfied if they'd just stop scratching them, but how can you expect someone who's itching to death not to scratch? And I'd love to go to bed just one night and not be wakened by either Ben or Carl around three in the morning." She sighed again. "Poor kids!" she said, shaking her head.

"But didn't the doctor do *anything*?" Katie watched her mother as she crumbled the cookie into little pieces onto the table. Her hair was askew and there were dark shadows under her eyes. Mrs. Collicut was pretty, with delicate even features, a small straight nose, and a wide happy smile when it was in working order.

And then she did smile. "Well, yes, he did." She gave a short laugh. "I'm sorry, Katie. The oldest always gets all the flack. I shouldn't unload my troubles on you. You're just a kid. I keep forgetting that."

"A pretty big kid," Katie reminded her.

"Yes. But . . . Anyway, the doctor found the twins severely allergic to about twenty-five things. Pollens. Dust. Dogs. A bunch of foods. You name it. Making meals for them is going to be really tricky. And the doctor's making up some kind of stuff so he can give them shots every week. He says it might work. *Might.*"

"Shots? Every *week*?

"Yes. Ben and Carl aren't too crazy about the idea either. But if it helps, maybe they won't mind so much."

"That means a trip across town to Dr. Ogilvy's fifty-two times a year. Waiting for the bus and all — and transferring."

"I know," said their mother. "Oh, well."

"Sometimes I can take them," said Katie, and then right away wished she hadn't. She could just see herself waiting for the bus in the rain. It seemed that it always rained in Halifax on days when people had doctor or dentist appointments. She'd have to keep Ben and Carl from running off in six different directions, transfer to the second bus, walk the five extra blocks to the clinic, nag the twins not to scratch. Imagine getting on a bus with two kids, identical right down to their bloody faces! Also, she really didn't have much extra time, with all the practising she had to do, plus a music lesson every week.

"Well," she said, "at least they're twins. Neither one of them is in this mess alone."

"That's what I often think now about our family," said Mrs. Collicut, almost as though she were talking to herself. "We've got each other for comfort and help."

Katie stared at her. "Got each other for *what*?" she demanded.

"For comfort and help . . . " repeated Mrs. Collicut, her voice trailing off. She sat up straight from her slumped position, looking startled.

"Comfort and help about *what*?" persisted Katie.

Mrs. Collicut got up from the chair and started to bustle about, tying on an apron, bringing a pile of things out of the fridge, turning on the stove. "Oh, nothing special," she said, sounding firm and cheerful again. "Often, people need comfort and help for small things, and it's nice to have lots of people around to give it." She flashed her wide smile at Katie before dumping some potatoes into the sink and turning on the tap.

Mr. Collicut appeared at the doorway, the

palm of his hand cupping his forehead. His mouth was drawn down at the corners as he said, "Hi, Ethel."

"Frank!" exclaimed Mrs. Collicut, the smile gone from her face. "You're home! I must have walked right by the car and not noticed. How long've you been here?"

He shook his head as though clearing it of a swarm of flies. "Oh, a while," he said. "Not long. Had a heck of a headache."

"But what is Mr. Giles going to . . . " began Mrs. Collicut.

Her husband banged the door jam with his fist. "Don't let me hear that man's name!" he shouted, and swung around to return to the TV room.

"Oh, dear," whispered Mrs. Collicut, following him. Katie could hear her murmuring, "Frank, dear, why don't you lie down until supper? You'll feel better when you get some food into you." Mr. Collicut shouted back something loud and angry.

Katie went over and continued to peel the potatoes that her mother had left. No practising tonight, I bet, she thought. Then she put down the knife and stared out the window. "Comfort and help," she repeated. "Comfort and help. I wonder . . . "

Chapter 2

The Collicut house was shabby, but it was large enough for both Katie and Daniel to have a room of their own. Katie's wallpaper was faded, with sprigs of violets on a white background that had become yellow with the passage of time. But the curtains were new, mauve with a deep ruffle, and there was a large hooked rug on the grey painted floor. On the bed was a patchwork quilt made by Mr. Collicut's mother. Every second square was mauve. On the walls, Katie had taped and tacked up pennants, maps, a picture of Beethoven with his large head and mop of hair, a photograph of her parents' wedding, posters of The Pink Panther, of Snoopy, of Michael Jackson, a large calendar, a sign that said I LUV NOVA SCOTIA.

"One thing about having dingy wallpaper," Katie once said to Julie. "You don't have to be careful of it." She knew friends who weren't allowed to put up a single thing on their walls.

Katie lay in her bed and listened to the morning sounds. She could hear the milkman thunking shut the milk chute. Mrs. Donovan's squawky dog was barking and barking, two streets over. A squirrel was chattering in the tree outside her window. The moan of a foghorn down by the harbour sounded muffled and far away. The rain had stopped, and she hoped that the bright light filtering in around her blind was a sign that it was going to be a fine day, and that the fog would burn off.

"Weather does things to me," she said, right out loud, and then snickered at herself. Just like old Miss Amery at the nursing home. Talking to myself like I was a hundred.

Sounds of footsteps in the kitchen came up through her bedroom register, and the opening of doors, water running. Katie checked her watch. 6:30. That meant her mother was preparing her father's breakfast. That also meant that he was going to work. She felt the knot in her chest — a familiar sensation lately — loosen.

Katie didn't need to get up for another forty minutes. That gave her a good half-hour of day-dream time. Would she pretend she was soft and curved-looking, dancing with Olaf Hensen at the graduation dance? Or how about her Festival dream with Chopin and the standing ovation? No, she'd done that one yesterday. She flipped over on her stomach and closed her eyes, pressing the side of her face into the pillow. I'll just remember for a while, she decided.

Once the memories started coming, it was hard to stop them. She remembered way back to the year they had won money in a lottery and spent it on a holiday at the beach. She was five then and Daniel was three. The twins weren't even born yet. The picture wasn't always clear and there weren't many details, but the memory seemed to be coloured in shining gold.

Katie smiled into her pillow, recalling the summer heat, the sunsets over that huge rocky island, the yellow surface of the sea in the morning light, the soft colour of the granite and of the sand. Even her hair was yellow way back then. Did it ever rain that week? If so, she couldn't remember. But she did recall her dad playing ball with them on the beach and helping them with their sandcastles, while her mother lay on the sand in her new swimsuit. She could remember exactly the way it looked. Blue with white straps.

The best memory of all was of herself — so high, so safe — riding on her father's shoulders as he carried her out through the waves.

But there was more. When Millicent Haggerty had thrown Katie's new doll down the cellar steps, her father had taken her by the hand and walked her all the way down to Point Pleasant Park. There he'd found a bench overlooking the open sea, and sat down on it, taking her up on his lap. She'd cried and cried, and he'd just held her and stroked her shoulder, gentle and comforting. She couldn't remember how old she'd been then, but it must have been pretty young. She could still feel the mixture of things she had felt in her father's arms that day: awful grief for her broken doll, comfort, warmth, love, a sense of sad completion.

Katie turned over on her back and watched the light grow on the ceiling. Then there was the time she had been chosen to play the piano during the intermission at the Christmas concert, the year she was eight years old.

Her mother had been sick in bed with pneumonia, but her dad had taken Daniel and her by the hand and walked over to the school in the snow, acting as though it was the greatest treat he'd had in years. He'd sat in the very first row, wearing his navy blue suit. And a tie. After she'd played, he'd gone right on clapping after everyone else had stopped. On the way home, they'd all gone for ice cream at McCulloch's Drive-In. He'd ordered a triple-decker for each of them, because it was such a special night.

"I love him so," whispered Katie.

The sound of angry voices shocked her out of her dream and she held her breath, listening. " . . . great moment to choose to burn the toast . . . late already . . . Mr. Giles can't stand . . . "

Then, "Murmur, murmur, murmur." That would be her mother.

"Then get a new one! Or get it fixed or something!" His voice was rising.

"Murmur, murmur, murmur."

"Don't you throw money in my face again! Can I help it if I don't make enough?"

"Murmur, murmur."

"Oh, forget it! Just forget it!" Katie could hear the kitchen chair being hauled out from the table.

"Murmur, murmur."

"I don't want it now! Eat it yourself! I'm late already!" *Slam*! The engine started, and Katie heard the car move off down the street.

She closed her eyes and dug her nails into her palms. Rehearsing again, she whispered, "Listen, Dad. We don't look for any miracles from you any more. All that tender comforting stuff was great, but we've learned how to get along without it. But I've watched you with the customers at the store. So cheerful, so smiling, so *polite*. That would suit us fine. In fact, we'd settle for just polite and nothing else. Try it," she chanted aloud. "You'll like it."

* * *

At breakfast, Katie could tell her mother was upset by the little round bump on her cheek that throbbed up and down, up and down. She's clenching her teeth, I bet, thought Katie as she sat down. But when her mother spoke, she sounded brisk and cheerful.

"It's a great day after the rain. Don't forget your music stuff, Katie. This is your Tuesday lesson. Ben. Carl. Please," she said to the twins. "Try not to scratch. I know it's hard. Daniel, is that all you're going to eat? A track star needs some fuel for all that running. And kids . . . "

"Yeah?"

"A new family moved into the corner house yesterday morning. I think there's a little girl. Or maybe a boy. How about calling for her?Or him. It's hard starting at a new school all alone. The yellow house."

"Okay, Mom." The three boys were already at the back door. "Bye!"

"Hey!" called out their mother. "Your teeth!"

"No time!" yelled Daniel, and he called back to Katie, "Get a move on! We'll wait for you at the corner."

Katie rose from the table and dumped her dishes on the counter. Then she brushed her teeth at the kitchen sink. It's not that I'm a browner, she argued to herself. It's just that I have kind of nice teeth and they might come in handy if I'm ever going to snare Olaf Hensen.

Before she left, she wanted to say something comforting to her mother, but she didn't even know how to begin. So she just went up to her, touched her briefly on the cheek, and gave her a hug. Then she picked up her books and her music and was gone. "See ya, Mom!" she called out. "Hang in there!"

* * *

The twins were already far ahead when Katie caught up to Daniel at the corner. They'd seen the new kid on the veranda, and known she wasn't their territory. A girl, and old. Maybe twelve or thirteen.

"Hi!" yelled Katie to the figure on the porch. "Wanta come with us? We're your neighbours. That white house back there in the middle of the block."

"The one that needs paint?" said the girl as she joined them.

Katie paused before answering. "I guess so. But who cares? I'm Katie and he's Daniel. He's on the track team. I'm in grade nine. I like music. What's your name? Do you like anything special? Where'd you come from?"

They were walking along towards school now, swinging their jackets. The sky was clearing and they could feel the warm September sun on their heads.

"Rita," said the new girl. "My name's really Marita, but that's too complicated for anyone except my grandmother. And no, I don't like anything special. Except maybe Winnipeg. Where I come from. Where I don't live any more. It's sunny a lot out there. And people are friendly."

"Well," said Katie, "*we're* friendly. And the sun's shining today. Or it's starting to, anyway."

"About time!" snorted Rita. "We've been living in a motel for almost a week and it's rained *every single day*."

"What grade are you in?" asked Katie, already hoping it wasn't nine.

"Eight," said Rita. Katie smiled.

"Okay, then. We'll take you up to your home-room. Your teacher's real nice. Mr. Johnston. And handsome. My teacher's Mrs. MacDonald."

Daniel was running now — ahead of them, back towards them, around them.

"What on earth is your brother doing?" frowned Rita.

"Training. For the track meet. In June."

"In *June*! But it's only September 15th." Then she looked hard at Daniel as he loped back to join them. "He'll probably *need* all that time if he wants to win anything. He's so short."

"But fast," snapped Katie. "You don't have to be slow just because you're small."

"Maybe. But his legs are so short he'll have to run twice as fast as everyone else just to keep up."

Daniel was walking along beside her, panting. He was biting his nails, and the tic in his eyelid was jumping again.

"I wouldn't even start anything," went on Rita, "if I didn't know right from the start that I was going to be the winner."

It was Katie's turn to take a long hard look at Rita. She was dark and slender, and her hair had that bounce and roundness that's the mark of natural curl. Katie ran her palm down her own straight, sandy hair. Nothing-coloured, she often called it. Rita's skin was creamy and smooth, and she already seemed to be a little bit curvy in the right places.

"You twelve?" asked Katie.

"No," replied Rita. "Thirteen, almost fourteen."

"Same as Katie," said Daniel. "But she skipped a grade. That's why she's ahead of you."

"Oh, Daniel," growled Katie. "Shut *up*!"

"Ah!" Rita smiled, with an odd twist of her lips. "So! A *brain*."

"No, I'm *not*," retorted Katie. "They just took a third of class one year and pushed us a little faster — just to see what would happen. Like guinea pigs. My dad wanted me to be in that group, so I stayed." She sighed. "But I find it really hard. I missed all my multiplication tables, and still count on my fingers half the time. In secret. I keep my hands under my desk." She chuckled. "Just ask my teacher if I'm a brain. She'd laugh till she cried."

They were at the schoolyard now, and the kids were spilling in off the sidewalks. Katie pointed out several people who'd be in Rita's class, and told her a little bit about them. "That's Alice. She collects stamps. She's really serious. But nice. There's Joe Simpson. He's a barrel of fun and drives the teachers crazy. Over beside the jungle gym is Sally Gormier. She's got a hearing aid, but she gets real mad if you mention it. So don't. She hears fine."

Suddenly, from Rita, "Hey! Who's *that*?"

Katie's heart lurched and she felt a strange hiccup in her chest. "That's Olaf Hensen. He's in

grade *nine.*" *My* class. Not yours. She looked at
Rita's curly hair, her milky skin. Oh darn, she
thought.

"Ever *gorgeous!*" breathed Rita. "My mom
says you can't possibly be in love at age thirteen,
but she's wrong. I've been in love four times since
grade five." She grabbed Katie's arm. "What's he
like?"

Katie looked at Olaf's mop of thick black
hair, his strong face, his sure way of moving.
"Okay, I guess," she said.

"Does he have a girlfriend?"

Katie paused before she answered. "No," she
said. She thought about that. He's really nice to
me. He calls me Taffy. In about fifteen years I
want to marry him and have a bunch of black-
haired kids. He's mine and you can't have him.
But no. He doesn't have a girlfriend.

Katie took Rita up to her homeroom and
introduced her to the teacher. After that she went
down to the schoolyard and talked to her best
friend, Julie, till the bell rang. She always hated
first period — another hour-long struggle with
math. She sighed, and then smiled. Today was
Tuesday. Her music lesson. Whatever else rose
up in life to slap her in the face, she could always
count on Tuesdays. Tuesday afternoons never
failed her.

* * *

As she set off for the conservatory at 3:30, Katie

thought about the piece she was working on — a Bach gavotte — and hummed it as she walked. Humming the quick parts was tricky, and she had to add a lot of dum-di-dums. People smiled at her as she passed, because she looked so happy and also so funny.

Her left arm was wrapped around her music and books, but her right hand was out in front of her, playing the treble part of the piece, even the runs. And she was walking in time to the music.

When she reached the conservatory, she stopped outside to listen to the familiar din coming through the open windows. The combination of pianos and violins and voices, melodies and scales and high soprano trills, made a sound close to total discord. But her heart always lifted when she heard it.

One day she had taken Julie's tape recorder down with her and recorded twenty minutes of that sound. She had no cassette recorder to play it on, but she figured she could listen to it every day in her old age, when she'd be too full of arthritis to play the piano any more. She kept the tape in her bureau drawer under her T-shirts.

As always, the lesson did not fail her. Madame Gagnon was pleased with her progress. She clapped her hands and gave her a little hug. "*Ma chère enfant,*" she cried when Katie finished the Bach, "you have work very hard and have establish the spirit of the piece. And your runs are very clear and crisp." She paused. "Katie . . . "

"Yes, Madame?"

"Is there any way your family could manage two lessons a week? I know it is much money, but you have a big talent. I do not like to see such a talent lie around without *beaucoup de* development."

"I don't think so, Madame," sighed Katie. "We've got four kids in our family. And the twins have rashes and need a lot of drugs and things — expensive stuff. I don't think my dad makes much money, else why does he talk about it all the time? And why has the house needed paint for about five years now? I wouldn't even want to ask." She stopped talking and screwed up her eyebrows. "Not right now, anyway."

"Not right now?"

"No. I can't explain, Madame Gagnon. It's just not a good time to raise any dust in our house."

"Dust?"

"Not a good time to ask for anything complicated. And this is pretty complicated."

Madame Gagnon sighed. "You are my best student, Katie. I don't want you to — how you say it? — wither on the vine."

Katie laughed. "Don't you worry, Madame Gagnon. I'm not going to wither on any vine. You just wait and see."

As Katie walked home, she jumped from happy to sad, from excited to depressed inside her head. Happy to be Madame Gagnon's best pupil, sad that the Collicuts weren't rich and that the twins were covered in itchy and expensive rashes. Excited that Madame wanted to give her an extra lesson each week, depressed that she couldn't even tell them about this at home right now.

When she walked up the alleyway to her house, she passed her father's car and knew he was home.

"Please let him be happy today," she whispered.

Chapter 3

Supper was okay that night. There were no fireworks. Mr. Collicut didn't talk. He sighed quite a few times, but he didn't scold anybody, didn't criticize, didn't even mention the undercooked potatoes, which were really pretty awful. Mrs. Collicut talked a lot, asked questions about school and laughed extra hard when there was a joke.

The twins sat there scratching, and pushing their carrots under their potatoes.

If you're a twin, wondered Katie, does that mean you *both* hate carrots?

Their father didn't even notice. He just kept his eyes on his plate, only raising them once in a while to stare off into space.

Katie got through to him once, though. "Hey, Dad," she said.

"Hmm?"

"This afternoon, Madame Gagnon said that I was her best pupil."

He looked up and smiled. "Nice going," he said, but his eyes were dull and he didn't say anthing else.

Katie's mother fluttered away in the background, exclaiming how wonderful it was about Madame Gagnon, how proud she felt, how happy she was for Katie. But Katie hardly heard. By now she knew that almost every move she made pleased her mother. It was her dad who she wanted to be proud, to make a big fuss over her. I want, she thought, as she twisted her napkin, to be carried through the waves on his shoulders again. But no. He'd returned to his contemplation of his dinner plate. Katie took a deep breath.

Well at least I was luckier than Daniel, she reflected. At least he didn't ask me why I hadn't done better. *"Nice going."* Could be a whole lot worse.

Mr. Collicut left the table as soon as he'd finished eating, without so much as an *excuse me*. Katie nibbled slowly on her chocolate chip cookie and looked at her father's half-eaten dinner. Mrs. Collicut was still chattering on about her day, the Hanley's new baby, the weather report, the O'Hara's crazy marmalade cat. Katie reached over and patted her arm.

"It's okay, Mom," she said. "Stop pretending everything's rosy. It isn't. Let's just eat our apple sauce and get the dishes done. I've gotta do my practising. Julie's coming over to help me with my math when I'm finished."

Twenty minutes later, Katie was seated in front of the piano. She touched the keyboard with both hands and thought, *silent*, all silent. And it's me that's going to make music come out of it.

She knew she should start with scales, with finger exercises, but tonight she needed real music. Tonight, she thought, I'll be easy on myself. I'll give me a treat. I'll skip all that sensible stuff.

So for an hour Katie played all the pieces she knew by heart, then opened up book after book and played compositions in them that she was familiar with. Mostly she chose peaceful music with no jarring tonal combinations, no thundering chords.

Playing it, she felt as though she were floating on some steady barge, slithering down a safe, slow-moving river. When she finished, she rose from the bench and patted the piano lovingly. As she turned toward the door, she saw her father sitting on a chair in a dark corner. He was smiling at her.

"Thank you, Katie," he said.

"For what?"

"For all that peaceful stuff. It helps."

Helps what?

Then her father spoke again. "You're lucky," he said.

"Lucky?"

"Yes. To be able to do that. I'd give anything right now to be able to sit down and make music like that."

Right now?

"You could, you know," said Katie. "You're musical. I've seen you dance with Mom in the

27

kitchen." *But not for a long time, I haven't.* "You just need some lessons."

Mr. Collicut sighed and then laughed a little. "That's a pretty tough trick for an old dog to learn," he said. "I think we'll settle for one musician in this family."

* * *

That evening, Julie and Katie worked on math. The session went well. "Gee, Julie," said Katie. "Thanks. I'm starting to feel like I might even understand this sometime. Maybe in about twenty years."

Julie grinned. She was overweight and shy. She'd gladly have traded her math skills for a chance to look like Katie. All that long straight hair, the colour and sheen of pulled taffy, and those big brown eyes. And *slim*.

"Julie," said Katie, "I really wish I could give you something for all your work. You've been here every single night since school started. Anything I can help you with? Give you music lessons or something?"

Julie frowned. "Just a sec, I'm thinking." Then she chuckled and said, "Yeah. I know what. Make me thin. In fact, make me thin in time for the June graduation dance. In time for someone to like what they see and ask me to go." She laughed again. "What a hope!" She stared at her stomach, and put her hand up to touch her double chin. She certainly wasn't laughing now.

Katie looked at her thoughtfully for a moment. In her imagination she sliced off the stomach, thinned down the chubby arms, got rid of the extra chin. Pretty! That's what Julie was under all the fat. She'd never realized it before. Suddenly she was excited.

"Lookit, Julie," she said, bending forward from the edge of the bed and pointing at her, "it's not like you're a *monster* or anything. You don't have to lose two tonnes, or even fifty kilograms. I betcha twelve kilos would do it. After all, you're pretty short."

Katie stood up, her mind suddenly made up. "Okay, pal!" she announced. "You're on! You get me through the final June math exam, and I'll make you thin in time for the graduation dance."

Julie looked hopeful and scared all at the same time. "But what'll I have to *do*?" she asked. "Not stop *eating*?"

"Don't be dumb, Julie," said Katie. "You're not gonna starve to death. We won't make you into one of those anorexia people. But you're not gonna live on potato chips and chocolate bars any more, either."

Julie threw herself down, stomach side up, on the bed. "Me and my big mouth!" she wailed.

"You and your big mouth is right," laughed Katie. "And what you're gonna learn is when to open it and when to shut it."

Julie just groaned.

"Like open it for lettuce and cucumbers and

cottage cheese," went on Katie. "And shut it for lemon meringue pie and six cans of pop a day."

Julie flopped over onto her stomach, mumbling into the pillow, "I'm dying! I'm dying!"

"*Well*?!" Katie sounded stern.

Julie sat up on the bed. "By June, you said?"

"By May 31st. That'll give some guy time to notice how gorgeous you've become."

Julie took a long shuddering breath and closed her eyes. "*I'll do it!*" she announced. "But *how*? And *what*? And *where*?"

"Listen, Julie," began Katie, speaking fast. She was excited. "I heard about a man who lost five kilograms in one year just by leaving sugar out of his coffee. That's all he did. We don't have a whole year. But if we cut all the junk out of your life, I bet we can work a miracle. Fish out that diet the doctor gave you and give it to me. I'm gonna be your personal policeman."

"Like how?"

"Like I'll make eating charts. Every day before I have my math lesson with you, you'll have to show me your chart. Every time you eat one peanut, one crumb, one slice of carrot, one finger-lick of frosting, one glass of milk, you'll have to write it down. You'll feel pretty silly writing 'four milkshakes' or 'six chocolate bars' or 'two dozen doughnuts,' or . . . " and Katie laughed, "I *hope* you'll feel pretty silly!"

"What else?"

Katie's mind was going clickety-click. "I'll

give you one treat per day. One cookie, maybe. Or one piece of cake if it happens to be your birthday. A small piece." Julie moaned. "But if you slip up even once on your diet, you'll lose your treat for the next day. *And* . . . " Katie aimed a fierce look at Julie.

"What?"

"You can't cheat. Everything on your chart has to be the truth. If I ever find you've cheated, I'll stop rescuing you that very day."

Katie went to the top drawer of her bureau and fished around in it. "Here!" she announced, holding up a dangling tape measure. "This is for later. Right now we're going downstairs to make you a farewell chocolate marshmallow sundae. I'll make it with nuts and a cherry and piles of goo."

"Farewell to what? You make it sound like a funeral or something."

"It'll be a farewell-to-fatness sundae. Eat it slowly, because it'll be your last until after the graduation dance. After you've eaten it, we're going to weigh you and measure you. And every Wednesday evening we'll do the same thing. Until you're breathtakingly beautiful."

Julie sat up straight on the bed and grinned. "Okay," she said. "I *will* do it. I'll probably never live to go to the dance, because I expect I'll die of misery long before that. But I'll do it."

Katie was over at her desk, hurriedly

making a couple of charts — ruling lines, marking in dates, times, categories.

"Here!" she said finally, handing them to Julie. "And there's a section on this page for exercise. At least twenty minutes a day — or else. You can use that exercise list that Miss Martison gave us. Days when she gives us a gym class, you can count it as one of the sessions. Hey! You know what, Julie?"

"What?"

"This is fun. If I don't get to be a famous concert pianist, I think I'll run a health club, a whatcha-call-it, a *spa*. We can use your before-and-after pictures for my advertisements. *Katie Collicut's Health Spa. From Fat to Fit in Five Fabulous Months. Guaranteed.*"

She took her camera off the bureau. Her grandmother had given it to her for her birthday and it had a built-in flash.

"Okay, Julie. Stand facing the camera and look as awful as you can. Stick out your stomach. Sag your shoulders. Pull down your chins so both of them show. Look *fat*. When we get this developed, you're going to stick it up on your mirror to give you courage."

"Katie?"

"What?"

"Katie, let's go downstairs first and make the sundae. I feel like I need a little comfort before all those awful things start to happen to me."

32

*   *   *

That night, Katie wrote an entry in the diary her father had given her for Christmas.

Dear Diary:

> Dad was pretty good today. You really notice a day when he isn't mad about something. But even when he's okay, he isn't exactly Fun City.
>
> I'm going to make Julie thin and she's going to make me smart in math. All before June. Could be tricky.

*   *   *

The next day was sunny again. Mr. Collicutt had left for work by the time Katie came down for breakfast. Rita called for her and Daniel just as they were putting their dishes in the sink. She looked cheerful.

"Almost like a day in Winnipeg," she said. "I could maybe start to like this place if we go on having weather like this."

On the way to school, Rita asked, "What does your dad do?"

"He works for a man who's a plumber. Dad keeps the books and records and stuff and answers the phone. Sells things in the store like faucets and pipes and nozzles. Orders stuff. There's just him and Mr. Giles and the four junior plumbers."

"Who's Mr. Giles?"

"He's Dad's boss. He's the chief plumber."

"Is he nice?"

"I don't think I should talk about that."

"Then I guess he's not nice. My dad's his own boss."

Katie kicked a rock. It went flying along the sidewalk and hit a tree. "Lucky guy," she said.

"Yeah. And he makes lotsa money."

"Doing what?"

"He's a salesman. Some days he sells so much that he just takes a day off for fun."

"Nice."

"Yeah. Is that why your dad's home from work so much?"

"Who told you that?"

"Our next-door neighbours, the Mullens. Mrs. Mullen says his car is in the alleyway half the time."

"He has awful headaches lately. That's why. And it's none of Mrs. Mullen's business. My dad works hard. He says he's three people at work — a clerk, a bookkeeper, and a secretary — and sometimes a cleaning lady. That makes four. He says they need at least two more people. And Mr. Giles . . . "

"What about him?"

"*Nothing*. C'mon. We're gonna be late for school."

"Well, excuse *me*! I was just asking."

"C'mon, Rita. *C'mon*".

Chapter 4

When Katie, Daniel and Rita reached school, they found a big poster in the front hall. In large letters, it said:

PLAY AUDITIONS ALL THIS WEEK

FOR

THE CLOWN WHO CRIED

Come and try out for the parts.

After 3:30 in the General Purpose room.

Rehearsals

will

be

Tuesdays and Thursdays

at 4:00 p.m.

"Katie?" Daniel's eyes were wide.

"What?"

"I'm gonna do it! I'm gonna try out. Someone told me that play was real funny. When I went to Cub camp two years ago, I had a funny part in a play and everyone was in stitches."

"You're kidding!" cried Rita. "You don't seem one bit like a funny kid to me."

Dan was biting his nails again. "No," he said. "I'm not. I'm too shy. But I'm funny *inside*. And in a play you're really someone *else*, so you're not shy any more. It's just exactly like . . . what? . . . I know, like stepping right into someone else's skin."

Daniel's face was serious but bright as he headed for his homeroom. Track practice was late today because the coach, Mr. Jemseg, had a dental appointment. Dan could go to the auditions and still be ready at 5 for his training session. And the play rehearsals were on days when there were no track practices. He grinned. It was like a jigsaw puzzle with all the pieces fitting perfectly.

At recess, Daniel went to the school library and checked out a copy of the play. Reading as quickly as he could, he was able to see a clear picture of the character he wanted to be. He'd ask to try out for the part of the clown's son — awkward, bumbly, warm-hearted and a real nut. Inside his head, all through math period and French and noon hour and phys. ed. and science and social studies, he thought about how the son should move, talk, sit. At 3:25 he was outside the General Purpose Room, waiting. So were about forty-five other kids.

Daniel wasn't nervous. He didn't bite his nails. At camp, acting had just seemed to be something he was meant to do. It was as natural for him as breathing. And *fun*! It was like walking into a whole other world, and while you were there, forgetting your own real worries. You were somewhere else and somebody else and that was all that mattered.

They held the auditions for the biggest parts first, and it took a long time. A lot of kids wanted those parts. As Daniel watched and listened, he thought, someday I want to be a director. I can see all the things they're doing wrong. It would be fun to show them how to do them right. It'd be neat to take a bunch of kids and a play and put them together in a way that was perfect.

"Daniel Collicut!"

He jumped out of his thoughts and stepped forward.

"Trying out for what?"

"The clown's son."

"Okay. Here's the script. Get up there and let's see what you can do. Start at this line. I'll give you your cues. Know what a cue is?"

"Yes."

"Okay. Fine. Fire away."

Daniel started. It was a funny part. As he spoke the lines, he stalked about, used arm gestures, moved his mouth, his eyes, his whole head, in the ways he'd been inventing all afternoon. There were hoots of laughter from the kids when he said some of the lines, and he warmed to their response, getting funnier and funnier, more and more relaxed.

At last the director, Mr. Hamilton, said, "Okay, Daniel. That's it. You've shown us all we need to know. And Dan, I don't usually say this on the first day of auditions, but I don't expect we'll find anyone as good as you for that part. We'll do tryouts for the rest of the day, but I think it's yours. I'll know by the end of the afternoon. If we decide to give it to you, I'll call you at home this evening."

Daniel almost floated out of the General Purpose Room. He knew it was unfair of Mr. Hamilton to say those things before anyone else had tried out for the part. But he couldn't pretend he wasn't pleased. And excited. He was so fired up that he didn't even notice the time when he passed the school clock on the way to the playing field. It was 5:25.

When he arrived on the field, the kids were already practising, and Mr. Jemseg was standing around thumbing his stopwatch and yelling at people.

"Harder! Harder! Try harder! Move those legs!"

When he saw Daniel, he came right over to him, hands on hips, his face grim.

"And you, Daniel Collicut! D'ya think being on the track team is some kind of tea party you can come early or late to, however it suits your fancy? Listen, kid, any more of this dilly-dallying and you're *out*! Understand?"

"I'm sorry, Mr. Jemseg, but I —"

"I'm not interested in your excuses. If it was your mother's funeral or if you had triple pneumonia, okay. Anything less, I don't wanna hear it. Get it, kid?"

"Yeah. Yeah, sure."

Daniel stepped onto the track and started doing laps. He didn't know whether it was excitement over the play, or fear of Mr. Jemseg, but he felt a new kind of energy. His legs moved as though they had wings, and he knew he was running faster than he ever had before. When he finished the second lap, he slowed to a walk and Mr. Jemseg came up to him.

"Dan," he said, "I don't know which'd make me more mad at you today — if you were slow or if you were extra fast. But you were fast just now, kid, really fast. Anyone as good as that doesn't come strolling in at 5:25 for a five o'clock practice. Don't let it happen again!"

"No."

"Okay. Let's see you do it one more time."

* * *

Daniel burst into the house at suppertime yelling, "Dad! Dad! I did my best time yet!" But his mother came racing out to the back door with her finger to her lips.

"Sorry, Dan," she said, her voice low, "but your dad's been home since noon. He's in bed with another headache. Keep down the yelling, eh? I'm glad to hear you did well, and your dad will be so proud. But wait'll he wakes up on his own."

Daniel walked into the dining room and took

39

his seat. Like a funeral party, he thought. Even the twins were silent. He looked at Katie across the table and threw her a question with his eyebrows. She just shook her head, cast her eyes upward, and then returned to her lamb chop.

Finally she put down her fork and said to her mother. "Mom, I'm sorry, but can I heat it up later? I'll do the dishes then, too." She got up from the table, took her plate out to the kitchen and put it in the fridge. Then she went into the living room and sat down at the piano bench.

She felt like a volcano all ready to erupt, a bomb about to burst. No peaceful music for her tonight. What she needed was to pound the piano with her scales, her arpeggios, her fast finger exercises — hard and furious — until she got some of the tension out of her system, until she felt the hard knot in her stomach untie itself and relax. She put her fingers on the keys and started. Up and down the keyboard they travelled — firm, skilful, with increasing speed. She did scales for every note, singly and with both hands. Then she started into her arpeggios. Up and down, up and down, louder, stronger. As she played, her mind moved into her fingers and away from her tensions.

"*STOP IT!*" The voice was like a clap of thunder and it came from away upstairs in her father's room. "Ethel! Make her stop! I can't stand that racket!" and then, more faintly, she heard him add, "Please, please make her stop!"

Katie's hands dropped into her lap and she sat perfectly still, scarcely breathing. She listened to her mother rush up the stairs and then the *murmur, murmur* of her voice as she spoke to her father. She could hear the sharp irritation of her father's voice, but not what he was saying. Katie continued to sit in front of the piano, not moving.

Finally, after about ten minutes, Mrs. Collicut came downstairs, very slowly. She went into the living room and sat down on the bench beside Katie and put an arm around her shoulders.

"Mom," said Katie, voice trembling, "he can't stand the noise, or anything else. I'm getting so I can't stand *him*." She turned agonized eyes to her mother. "Mom, stop protecting him. Protect *us* for a change. We live here, too."

Mrs. Collicut put her hand over her face, and Katie realized to her horror that her mother was crying. She fumbled in her jeans pocket and pulled out a crumpled tissue. "Here," she said. Mrs. Collicut took it, wiped her eyes and blew her nose. Then she took a deep breath.

"There!" she said. "That feels better. I've been needing to do that for a long time. Parents" — she chuckled a little — "should be allowed a good cry at least once a week."

Mrs. Collicutt looked at Katie. "It's no fun trying to be strong *all* the time."

"Well, why doesn't *he* try to be strong more often?"

Her mother sighed. After a long pause, she seemed to make up her mind. "Listen, Katie," she said slowly, "can you please try to understand at least a little of what I'm going to say?"

"Oh, gosh, Mom, *sure*. I'm just so sick of you never telling us anything. And of Dad telling us too much."

"Well, okay then. How about we try and put ourselves in your dad's shoes? He's intelligent and he's got a lot of talents. Right?"

"Right."

"Well, in spite of all those brains and talents, somehow or other your father wound up wasting them."

"What do you mean, 'wasting?'"

"He was athletic, and everyone thought he was going to set the world on fire with his running. Then when the accident wrecked his knees, all those hopes and dreams went down the drain."

"I know," Katie interrupted wryly. "So he keeps telling us."

"Try not to be too hard on him, Katie. Did you also realize that he's very musical?"

Katie blushed and shook her head.

"Where do you think you got *your* talent from? Certainly not me. I'm tone deaf. So what happened to him?

"What?"

"That musical talent was wasted too. He put all his eggs in one basket because he believed — and still does — in total commitment to his main goal. At that time, this meant pouring all his efforts into running. Then when he couldn't run any more, he felt he was too old to start music lessons." Mrs. Collicutt looked at Katie and smiled. "It means a lot to him that you do so well with your music. It's like a second chance for him."

"Anything else?"

"Yes, lots. Worst of all, his brains were sort of wasted too."

"His brains?"

"Yes, brains. He did really well at school. He'd planned to work summers after he was through school, and go to university."

"Well, why didn't he?"

"Because when he was still young — too young, nineteen years old — he fell in love with an irresistible woman" — Mrs. Collicutt grinned her wide grin — "and married her. In order to support this wonderful lady, who became almost instantly pregnant, he took — *temporarily* — a really awful job in a plumbing supply and repair store. A big store. The plumber, Mr. Giles, got to do the interesting work with his four apprentices while your dad did all the joe-jobs — sweeping the place, carrying heavy equipment, doing all the books, looking after the telephone and the store, putting in the orders, listening to all the customers' complaints. But that's not all."

"What else? I know all that other stuff."

"What else? We did a really stupid thing. We

were very young and hadn't a clue about money. So we bought a big house that we couldn't afford, and settled down to spend the next twenty years paying off the mortgage. We wanted a house so that we could fill it up with children. And I was no help with that mortgage because I was pregnant, and also not trained to do much of anything, anyway. Then when you were born, Katie, I wanted to stay home and look after you myself. And of course a year later Daniel arrived. It was as though every time we had a new baby we were so pleased we wanted to have another one right away."

"Right away?"

Mrs. Collicutt laughed. "Well we did have a big gap of time between you kids and the twins. Five years! By then we were thinking that maybe your dad could handle part-time work and part-time university and a third child. He wanted both an education and a big family, and it looked as though maybe we could have everything. But we didn't have a third child. We had a third and a fourth. Twins! That seemed to make your father twice as proud as if there'd been only one. But he hadn't counted on Mr. Giles expanding his business at just about the same time, without hiring any extra help in the shop. And neither of us expected *allergic* twins needing special tests, special drugs, special diets. By then we were a big family, filling up that big house your dad bought.

Six pairs of feet and six pairs of shoes and boots. Six winter coats."

"And piano lessons." Katie's face was bleak. Raining again, she noticed, as she stared grimly out the window. And there's that fog horn moaning, keeping me company.

"Yes. Piano lessons. But he, we *both* want that for you. That's part of why I don't want to talk about these things to you. I don't want you to feel *guilty*, or anything stupid. Maybe I should stop."

Still on the piano bench, Katie put her arm around her mother's waist. "Go on, Mom. I need to hear. I need to understand. Tell me more."

"Well, you already know that his job is too hard. I don't mean that it's too difficult, that he's not smart enough for it. In fact, all the parts of it are easy — so easy that they're often boring. I just mean that he really does need extra help. Your father spends his whole life hurrying because he's always behind in everything. There's just too much work for one person. I know this is true. He tells me all he does in the course of the day, and no one could do it faster or better. He never has any energy left over for courses or fun or even friends. Sometimes — *often* — he's too tired even to rest."

Katie thought that would be like having three times as much homework to do, with no time for Julie, or music lessons and practice, or for just looking at the autumn leaves or the winter snow or sunsets over the Northwest Arm.

"And he's young," added her mother. "It's not right to be exhausted the entire time when you're only thirty-three years old."

Well, Katie didn't think that was all that young, but she guessed it wasn't really elderly. She tried to think about being tired all the time, but she couldn't even imagine it.

"And . . . ?" she prompted.

"The last is the worst," sighed Mrs. Collicut. "It's Mr. Giles. He's got his own problems — a nagging wife, a stomach ulcer, a cross nature — and he takes them all out on your father. He scolds him all the time like he was a five-year-old kid, and criticizes him so much that your father says if he ever praised him he thinks he'd faint. And the things he scolds him for . . . "

"Like what?"

"Like being behind with his billing, or not having swept the office floor, or not having finished his bookkeeping for that day — all the things that happen because there's too much for one person to do. And when he tells Mr. Giles this, Mr. Giles threatens to fire him. So your dad has to just shut up all day, work a hundred kilometres an hour, hear nothing but *'growl, growl, growl,'* and then also worry about losing his job."

Katie thought about that supply teacher they'd had last year who'd taken a disliking to her. Everything Katie did seemed to be wrong,

46

even when she was trying hard to please her. The one time she'd tried to defend herself, the teacher had ridiculed her in front of the whole class. She remembered coming home from school that day. She'd snapped at Daniel every time he'd opened his mouth.

"And we only had her for two months," said Katie.

"Had who? *What*?"

"Never mind, Mom. And thanks for telling me this stuff. But can't he *do* anything about all this? Can't he *escape*? And what will Mr. Giles do if Dad keeps staying home all the time?"

Mrs. Collicut looked at Katie and her eyes were very sad. "I don't know the answer to any of your questions, Katie," she said. "I don't know any escape route for a man who has to support a wife and four children. And no, I don't know what Mr. Giles will do if your dad keeps staying home so much."

"Mom?" It was Daniel at the door to the living room.

Mrs. Collicut swung around. Daniel sounded scared. "Yes?"

"I just went into Dad's room to tell him about the play. Mr. Hamilton phoned a few minutes ago to tell me I got that part. Dad was just lying on the bed staring at the ceiling. I went over and spoke to him, but he didn't even notice I was there."

Mrs. Collicut went right upstairs. Katie

47

walked to the kitchen, got her plate out of the fridge and dumped the contents into the garbage. Then she stacked the dishes and put the food away. When she started running the water into the dishpan, she found Daniel beside her.

"I'll dry," he said.

Funny, thought Katie, as she handed Daniel the eggbeater, we used to fight a lot. But it seems like right now we need each other too much to bother with that kind of foolishness.

Chapter 5

The next morning, Katie and Daniel found it hard to understand what was going on. It was as though yesterday had never happened. When they went down to the kitchen to have breakfast, there was their father getting ready to leave the house.

"Hi, kids!" he said, his face peaceful and his smile warm. "Another glorious fall day!" He came over and gave each of them a hug, and planted a kiss on the tops of both twins' heads as they bent over their cornflakes.

"Those rashes look better!" he grinned, leaning over to peer into their faces.

"Well," he announced as he kissed Mrs. Collicut goodbye, "I'm off! Have a good day!"

"Well!" exclaimed Katie, when the door closed behind him. "What was all that?"

Their mother's smile was wide and her face relaxed. "He had a good night's sleep. Lately he's been tossing and turning half the night."

Katie thought about that. Before her math exam in June the year before, she'd been awake hour after hour, fretting. The next day, she'd felt like a squashed banana peel.

"Gee!" she said. "Mom, does he *often* sleep like that? Like, I mean, *not* sleep?"

"Most nights," said her mother.

* * *

Katie and Daniel talked on the way to Rita's house.

"I wanted to tell him about the play," said Daniel, "but I decided to save it till tonight. If he's acting gloomy, it might be just the thing to perk him up." Daniel looked thoughtful. "And maybe make him proud of me," he added.

It was a dazzling late September day. The air was cool, but there was a clarity and a brightness to it that is typical of autumn in Nova Scotia. In the distance they could see a strip of brilliant blue, which was Halifax Harbour, and the air was full of white gulls riding on the updraughts.

"I don't know why Rita doesn't love it here," said Katie. "I can't imagine a nicer place to live."

But when they picked up Rita, she talked of other things: how much she missed her friends in Winnipeg; how many hills you had to climb in Halifax; how handsome Olaf Hensen was (*good grief*, thought Katie); how much money her father made last week.

Finally she said, "My mom says your dad looks just terrible. I don't mean ugly — he's a handsome guy for someone who's so old — but sick. She keeps saying, 'That man looks just *awful*.'"

Well, thought Katie, there goes my good mood. Thanks. Thanks a lot.

But Katie's spirits picked up throughout the day. At recess, she talked with Julie about her diet, and arranged to meet her that night for math and for checking the food charts.

For lunch, Julie ate a hard-boiled egg, carrot sticks, an apple and milk, instead of chips and a bag full of doughnuts.

"I can't believe it!" she cried. "I've lost a pound already."

"Well, I can," chuckled Katie. "Believe it, I mean."

In the afternoon, Daniel met with the director of the school play. "Here's your script, Dan," he said, holding out a sheaf of papers. "Study the cues, think hard about the character, and let's see how you do next week. By then we'll have chosen all the parts, and can start rehearsals." He smiled. "You were darn good yesterday. The faster you memorize the lines, the sooner you can concentrate on expression and movement."

All day long, Daniel kept thinking ahead to the moment when he'd tell his father about the play. He kept imagining his dad's face lighting up with joy and pride.

Even though he was only eleven years old, Daniel knew he'd discovered exactly what he wanted to do with his life. He was going to be an actor — rich and famous. He'd perform in Shakespeare's plays way up in Stratford, Ontario; he'd be on the CBC; he'd do movies too, moving in and out of a Hollywood penthouse.

As he had read the lines yesterday, he'd had a strange new feeling of things being absolutely right. And exciting. And oddly peaceful, too.

This must be what Katie feels about her music, he thought.

When Daniel arrived home, his father's car was still not in the alleyway. Good! No headache. Tonight at suppertime he'd make his announcement. He went up to his room to memorize his lines so that he'd have the evening free to do his homework.

At six o'clock, he heard his mother call out, "Supper's ready!" and he tore downstairs to join the family. He didn't look at anyone or realize how quiet they all were. As soon as they were seated at the table with the plates of food in front of them, he exploded.

"Dad!" he almost shouted.

"Not so loud, Daniel. Please," said his mother.

Katie was trying to send him hand and eye signals, but he was blind to everything she was doing.

"Dad!" he cried almost as loudly as the first time. "Listen. Yesterday there were auditions for a new play at school. Mr. Hamilton's the director. Sometimes he acts with Neptune Theatre, and is always real good. The play's called *The Clown Who Cried*, and is it ever funny!

"Anyway, I tried out for the part of the clown's son. Even at the tryouts everybody laughed and laughed. Dad, I was the very first person to audition for the part, and right away Mr. Hamilton said probably no one else would be as good as me. And, Dad?"

His father hadn't answered, but Daniel barrelled on. "Last night Mr. Hamilton called specially to tell me I had the part! How about that, eh?"

Daniel was leaning forward in his chair, his face eager.

Mr. Collicut's voice was low but even. "You're on the track team," he said, his jaw scarcely moving.

"Yeah, yeah. I know. But the practices are on different days. No problem."

Mr. Collicut had taken one bite of his supper; now he put down his fork. "I don't happen to think that spreading yourself thin is the way to succeed in life. I'm trying to stay calm, Daniel," — and he passed his hand across his eyes — "but I'll have to tell you that this is about the stupidest thing I've ever heard. How can you train for your running, practise for the play, and ever have two minutes left for your homework? If you want to be a great athlete, you've got to put your *all* into it. Not your half or your quarter. I know. I almost made it myself."

"But, Dad," pleaded Daniel, eyes stricken, "I don't really want — "

"Don't want *what*?" exclaimed Mr. Collicut, his voice rising. "You're on the track team, aren't you? The coach says you're fast. Well, get *faster*. Set your sights on something big. The provincial team. The national. And maybe more. Me — I dreamed of the Olympics until I injured my knees. And look where I ended up. Besides . . . "

"Besides, what?"

"Acting is sissy stuff. When you grow up, you don't want to end up prancing across a stage like an overgrown kid playing make-believe."

Mr. Collicut stood up. "*No!*" He was shouting now, banging the table. "You can't do it, and that's that!"

"But, Dad . . . " Daniel was scared to argue, but he had to. "I promised the director. And I've already learned my lines for the first scene."

"Well, *un*promise the director! And *un*learn your lines! For Pete's sake!" Mr. Collicut threw down his napkin and strode out of the dining room. They could hear him climbing the stairs, yelling, "Can't I ever come home to a peaceful house?"

Daniel felt as though someone had punched him in the stomach. There were so many feelings raging through him that he couldn't sort them out. He was both angry and sad — and wild with a sense of his own powerlessness. Was he really a sissy? Couldn't a person ever do two things without spoiling each one? Why did he have to be the best track star in the world?

All of a sudden he saw that if he won the provincial championship after the school meet, he'd be expected to win the national one. Then if he won that, he'd be shoved right onto the Olympic Team.

And suddenly he was aware of something else that he'd been pushing to the back of his mind for a long time. *He didn't like running.* He was just doing it to please his father. And now his dad wanted to take something away from him that Daniel *knew* was right for him.

He put down his fork and buried his face in his hands.

How could he do anything at all without making the director or the coach or his father mad? Who should he be loyal to? Which promises should he keep, which break?

His mind was spinning, spinning, spinning, like a top that had forgotten how to stop.

Katie stood up. "I'm sorry, Mom. I know this is the second night in a row that I haven't eaten my supper, but this is important. After our talk last night, I'm sorry for Dad, and I even understand things a lot better. But right now I'm sorrier for Daniel." She grabbed Daniel by the arm and gave him a yank.

"C'mon," she said. "We're going upstairs to talk."

Mrs. Collicut looked at the twins after Daniel and Katie had left. She gave a sad little laugh.

"Well," she sighed, "it certainly is great fun cooking meals these days. I hope *you're* hungry."

They were. Sometimes it seemed to Mrs. Collicut that Ben and Carl could slide right over the awful things that were going on in their house. It was as though, being twins, they lived in a little world all of their own. They hoed right into their supper and didn't scratch even once.

*　　*　　*

Upstairs, Katie headed for the bathroom because it was on the other side of the house from her father's bedroom. Sitting on the edge of the tub, she repeated a lot of the things her mother had told her the night before. As she talked, Daniel felt some of the anger ease out of him. But he was still hurt and sad.

"Isn't he *ever* going to be proud of me?" he asked Katie.

"He's proud right now," she said. "So proud, he can't stand the thought that you might stop running as fast as you do now."

"Well, okay. Maybe. But I'd like to hear it from *him*."

"Listen, Dan," grinned Katie, "you've just got to toughen up. That'd be a whole lot better than being scared and hurt. And more useful."

"Like how? And why?"

Katie stood up and put her hands on her

hips. But she kept her voice low. "Like I've got an idea. You'll have to be real tough and brave to do it, but if you want this acting thing enough, you *can* do it. If they told me I had to stop music because we were too poor, I'd clean out the city sewers each week to make money to pay for lessons. How much do you want to be in that play?"

"A *lot*. And if I go back on my word to Mr. Hamilton, I betcha he'll never ever give me a part again. How much do I want it? Like a hundred million times more than track teams or chocolate-covered doughnuts or a computer of my own."

"A*ha*!" said Katie, rubbing her hands together.

"Aha, what?"

"*Aha!* Meaning that's a lot of wanting. That's good. It means you can do it."

"Do what?"

"Do everything: what you want; what he wants; what the school wants — in *secret*."

"But *how*?"

"You don't have to lie. Just don't talk about the play. But *do* it. Lookit," Katie turned his shoulders around towards her, "when I get up early to practise, you're going to be out in your track suit running round and round the block. Learn your lines during recess and noon hour. Run to and from school twice a day. Do your homework in the evenings. It'll be rugged, and I'm sure there won't be much TV or Crazy Eights, but it won't kill you for just one year. Dad's probably right, it probably *is* too much to do under normal circumstances. But . . . "

"But?"

"But these are *special* circumstances. You promised the director you'd take the part. And the auditions for that part are all finished. If you don't do it, it'll really be unfair to him. And maybe it's good to be extra busy, and even tired, this year."

"Why?"

"Because it'll help keep your mind off some of the bad stuff that's going on around here."

For the second time in two days, Daniel could feel something new rising up inside of him. He'd always been shy and sort of nervous about things. He didn't feel that way now.

"Your idea is scary," he admitted to Katie. "But it doesn't scare me all that much. I guess that's because I'm more scared of losing that part in the play than I am of anything else."

Katie stood up. "And, Dan," she said, "if you're as good an actor as you say you are, Dad's going to come to that play and know you were really right to do it. And another thing . . . "

"Yeah?"

"He's gonna be proud. He likes strong people. Now. Let's go down and finish our supper. I'm hungry now. Let's hope she hasn't pitched it all in the garbage."

But she hadn't.

*   *   *

Katie didn't have much energy to write in her diary that night, so the entry was short.

Dear Diary:

You're lucky to be a diary. It's not much fun being people around here these days. If it isn't Rita growling about something, it's Dad being mad at one of us. Tonight it was Daniel who got it — for wanting to be in the play. But Dan's going to do it anyway. It was my idea. I didn't know he could be that brave. Or that I could be such a criminal.

Chapter 6

The days were starting to get cooler now, but the air was still brisk and cheerful. Those few hot, soggy days in September were long past, and along the railway cutting and across the Northwest Arm the leaves were starting to change colour. Occasionally they'd discover a whole tree that was almost completely turned — a scarlet splash of colour surrounded by greens and yellows. As Katie went on the long trek with the twins to their allergist, she watched the deepening fall with mixed feelings. Autumn in Nova Scotia was a bright and lovely time of year and she liked the energy that returned to her with the coming of fall. She loved walking through the fallen leaves, slurpy when they were wet, and light and crisp when they were dry.

But she found this time of year sad, too. It was the end of those long lazy days in the sun; of swimming in the Commons playground pool; of picnics in the Public Gardens beside the duck pond. Winter was ahead, with darkness descending at five o'clock in the afternoon, shivering waits for the bus on days she'd be going to the clinic with the twins, homework and math, and later, exams.

But if she just ignored what lay ahead, she could enjoy the bright leaves and the startlingly blue skies. She hummed a Chopin waltz as she came in the front door with Ben and Carl. Then, tossing her jacket on a hall chair, she went right into the living room to practise.

Suddenly her mother was beside her, putting a hand on her shoulder.

"Darling," she said, biting her nail, just like Daniel, "I'm going to have to ask you not to practise today."

"*What*? Mom! That's twice this week. I've got a recital coming up. And the Festival. There are fast parts in my pieces. I have to keep my fingers in good shape; otherwise they run away with me. You just can't skip days like that!"

"I know, I know." Her mother sighed and sat down on the bench beside her. "But I can't think what else to do. The doctor came this afternoon and said your dad had to have a really quiet house for a few days. He's giving him some medication to see if it'll help his poor old nerves."

"But *Mom*! What'll I *do*?"

Her mother put her fist over her mouth. "I'm glad I don't have ten kids," she said, ignoring the question. "Each one of you seems to have a really big problem right now, and I don't see any solutions growing on the trees."

She took a deep breath and went on. "To tell

you the truth," she said with a nervous little laugh, "I've got the odd problem myself these days."

Katie stood up. "Lookit, Mom. If this goes on, I'm gonna end up with soggy fingers and a mark of twenty-three out of a hundred in the Festival. And I can't see many signs of things getting much better around here. What's more, I'm not *gonna* get a mark of twenty-three. I'm going over to Madame Gagnon's to see if she has any brilliant ideas. If she hasn't, I'm gonna move that piano out to the corner of Inglis Street and Tower Road and practise on it there. Bye. See ya." Katie picked up her jacket and struggled into the sleeves.

"But your supper . . . "

"I'll grab a sandwich when I come home."

As Katie passed their little TV room on the way to the back door, she could see her father sitting on the old brown wicker chair. The TV was turned off. He was staring straight ahead, his hands in his lap. Even his fingers looked limp and exhausted.

* * *

Madam Gagnon was full of sympathy for Katie, and told her to cheer up. "It is not the finish of the world, *ma chérie*. But you must have a piano. That's for sure. I know it is fourteen blocks to my house, and I know also that you are a busy girl. But my piano, it sit empty and silent between seven and eight every morning. If you want it, it is yours. Here. I give you a key. So if I am sitting in my bubble bath when you will arrive, it will not be necessary that I jump out and let you in the door."

Katie felt as though she were four kilograms lighter. The fourteen blocks seemed like nothing. Besides, having to walk all that way meant she'd be leaving early in the morning. It would be great to miss the crowd in the kitchen burning toast, spilling juice, scrambling for lost socks or jackets or school books. Getting up around 5:30 would be easy compared to that.

"Oh, Madame!" she cried, hugging herself. "Thank you, thank you! I'm so relieved, I could die!"

Madame Gagnon laughed. "Well, *mon amie*, do not do anything so reckless as to die. It would spoil your piano technique." She gave Katie a little pat on the back. "It will give me very much pleasure to lend you my piano. Also I will be having real live music to entertain me at the breakfast."

The next morning, Katie didn't find it so easy, after all, to get up at 5:30. When the alarm went off, she felt as though she were three metres underground, struggling to get to the surface. Her eyes were almost shut as she dressed, and only after she'd washed her face with cold water did she start to feel one hundred per cent awake.

But when she went downstairs to get breakfast, Daniel was already there, dressed in his track suit, cutting up an orange.

"My new régime!" he grinned. "Three times around the block, and down to the bus stop and back. Or, sometimes, all the way up to the hospital and once around the grounds."

Katie felt better. If you have to feel miserable, it's nice to have company.

"I'm doing good," mumbled Daniel, his mouth full of cornflakes. "I'm getting faster, and the coach hasn't growled at me for a whole week."

Then he sobered up and put his spoon down. "Katie, he says he's gonna kill us all if we don't win the inter-school trophy. I hate all this win, win, win, stuff. When I'm out running in the morning I almost like it. It's nice to feel the wind in my face and the way I'm light and fast, like an animal running on the prairies. Why can't people just run because they *enjoy* it?"

"I dunno, Dan," Katie said, buttering her toast. "Sometimes I think it's okay to be in competitions. Like I want to win the Festival cup. I really think it makes me work harder. But some people just get nervous in competitions and go all to pieces. Everyone's different, I guess. Besides, I love music and want to be the best in the world. What about acting? If you were in an acting contest, how'd you feel?"

Daniel laughed. "I think I'd probably feel great. Already I'm hoping to get an Academy Award!"

Katie got seven out of ten in her math test that morning. This made her feel so good that everything in school seemed perfect to her: the sun streaming in the long windows; the smell of chalk and erasers and John O'Neil's bubble gum; Mrs. MacDonald's nifty new haircut; the hum of voices from the next room.

That seven on the page looked like a beautiful design drawn by a master artist. She glanced gratefully over to Julie and held up her paper. But Julie was frowning and looking out the window.

"Hey!" said Katie at recess, when she found Julie sitting behind the jungle gym on a pile of tires. "What's up? Why're you out here? And what's the big glumph all about?"

Julie took a long breath and let it out like a groan. "Katie," she said, "maybe we should stop this diet thing. I didn't even want to *see* you this morning, let alone speak to you. And you're my best friend."

"What on earth are you talking about?"

"Katie, listen. Don't be mad. Please. I pigged out yesterday on butter tarts. I *bought* them, for Pete's sake.

"How many?"

There was a pause. "Two dozen." Then Julie hid her face in her hands. Through her fingers she mumbled, "After I'd eaten the first five, I figured I'd blown the whole thing. So I ate the rest."

Katie just stopped herself in time from bawling Julie out and telling her she was a real dumb cluck.

This is another kind of competition, she thought. It's like wanting like crazy to win, but hating the things you have to do to get there — and knowing that the race is going to last for eight more months.

Katie put her hand on Julie's arm. "Lookit, Julie," she said, "forget the graduation dance. If you can, that is. Just take it a day at a time, like Mrs. Stein."

"What's Mrs. Stein got to do with it?"

"She's Daniel's homeroom teacher and she's trying to give up smoking. She told the class that when she thinks about not having a cigarette for a *year*, it's such a terrible thought that she goes right to her purse and hauls one out and smokes it. So she doesn't think about a year, she thinks about *today*. It wouldn't work for some people, but it works for her — and maybe you."

"Katie, I gained two pounds yesterday."

"Okay. Tough beans. That was yesterday. This is today. That was just one little binge. Relax! Cheer up!"

Julie sighed, but she also smiled. "Then you're not mad?"

"Mad, dummy? Why be mad? It's no fun teaching if you have a perfect pupil. This'll all be useful stuff for me to know when I open up my health spa."

*　　*　　*

When Daniel and Katie arrived home that noon, they saw the doctor coming out the door, black bag in hand, a frown on his face. At first he didn't see them, but then he cried out a hearty, "Hello, you kids! How's school?"

Too hearty, thought Katie as they both answered, "Hi. Fine."

Then Katie said, "How come you're here? How's my dad?"

The doctor paused before speaking again. "I'll leave it to your mother to answer all those questions," he said finally.

Good grief, thought Katie. Oh, good grief.

*　　*　　*

Inside the house, Mrs. Collicut was stirring their lunch soup, and sandwiches were laid out on the table.

Well, at least things *seem* pretty normal, thought Katie. She and Daniel both sat down and looked at their mother.

"Well?" asked Katie.

"Well, what?" Mrs. Collicutt said.

"What happened? Why was Dr. Haliburton here again? What did he say? He said to ask you."

Mrs. Collicut didn't speak as she poured the soup into bowls. Then she sat down at the table.

"Listen, kids," she said, "we have a little time to talk. Your dad's asleep. Dr. Haliburton gave him something to knock him out for a while. He was pretty upset when he came home from work."

She paused and looked out the window. The day that had started out so sunny and bright had turned foggy and wet. A slow fine rain was falling.

Intermittent drizzle, she thought, is what the Weatherman chooses to call it. I just call it dirty weather.

"The twins'll be home any minute," she sighed, "and the bare facts are too tricky for them to understand. So I'll just tell you the main stuff now, and we can talk more tonight after you've finished your homework and everyone's in bed."

"Well, hurry," said Katie, squirming in her chair and fiddling with her spoon.

"It's like this," began Mrs. Collicut. "Your dad has to quit his job at the plumbing store."

"*Quit!*"

"Yes, quit. The doctor says no human being should live the way he's been living for fourteen years. Doing the work of three men and all. Pushed to his limit every day of his life. And work he doesn't even like. Plus having Mr. Giles growl at him and scold him every hour on the hour. Not to mention worrying about getting fired. Better to quit."

She sighed again, then offered them her broad smile. "Don't you think that's a good idea?"

Katie and Daniel just looked at her. They didn't know what to say.

"Look." Mrs. Collicut started again. "Tell me something you both hate to do."

They thought for a moment. "Washing dishes," said Dan.

"Math problems," said Katie.

"Well," their mother said, "it would be a little like washing dishes and doing math problems as fast as you can, six days a week for fourteen years, and never ever being finished. Think about what that'd be like."

She paused while they thought. Then she went on. "And having someone stand around all the time saying you aren't doing it right, that you're too slow, that you're *no good.*"

"Gee, Mom," whispered Daniel.

Mrs. Collicut took a long tired breath. "So Dr. Haliburton says he *has* to stop working for Mr. Giles. And not next month, or next week. Right *now.* Your dad's going to go to work tomorrow and tell Mr. Giles. But first he needs a lot of sleep to help him find the strength to do it."

Katie and Daniel could understand most of what their mother was saying, but their minds were buzzing with unanswered questions. Daniel was biting his nails.

Finally Katie asked, "Does that mean he won't have a job? At all?"

"Where'll the money come from?" added Dan.

"How'll we pay for my music lessons?"

"How can we buy food?"

The questions were coming so fast that Mrs. Collicut couldn't even begin to answer them. Finally she spoke.

"Kids. Your questions are pretty hard, and I don't know all the answers. Besides, I can see the twins through the fog, just passing the Mullen's house. We'll have to wait till this evening to talk about it."

"But, Mom," said Daniel, "why did the *doctor* have to say all this? What's a *doctor* got to do with Dad's job?"

"Because your dad's a sick man, and the doctor's working on a way to make him better. Quitting work is one way."

"*Sick?*" Daniel was troubled. His father was as healthy as he was himself. He never seemed even to get a cold. Or flu. Or hayfever.

"Yes, sick," she said. "There are lots of ways of being sick."

"I don't believe it," insisted Katie. "He doesn't sneeze or have a fever does he?"

"You'll have to take my word for it, kids," said their mother, "until I have the time to explain it all tonight. But it's true. He's even going to have to go to the hospital for a little while to help him get better."

"The *hospital!*" The kids spoke together.

"Yes," she said. "The hospital. Now, here are

the twins at the door. We'll discuss this after they're in bed."

The door opened and the twins poured into the room, shouting the news of their morning's work in grade one.

"Hi, kids!" cried Mrs. Collicut, just as though everything were peachy-keen; just as though it weren't the end of the world.

Chapter 7

Katie and Daniel wondered if they could survive the suspense until the evening, when they'd be able to talk again with their mother. They drummed their fingers and shuffled their feet and looked out the window at the rain, while the twins babbled on about a Hallowe'en party they were planning in grade one.

Their mother asked questions about the party and made suggestions for costumes. She was very pale.

Katie thought, she can't be interested. Not *really*. Not with our whole world falling down around our ears.

Then they listened as Mrs. Collicut told the twins a watered-down version of their father's problem.

"He's so tired that he's sick," she said. "He'll have to go to the hospital for a while to get better, but he'll be fine before too long. If he seems cranky sometimes," she added, "it's just because he doesn't feel well."

"Like when the itching gets really bad," said Ben.

"When that happens, I could sometimes

punch a hole in the wall. Is it like that?" asked Carl.

"Something like that," said their mother.

She makes it sound so simple, thought Katie. For a moment she envied the twins because they were being protected from the whole truth, but then she felt a little stab of pride because she and Daniel were old enough to share the problem with their mother.

"Why don't you tell them to go get their pajamas on, Mom?" asked Daniel, his eyelid twitching again.

Mrs. Collicut laughed out loud. "It's only five o'clock, Dan. We haven't even had supper! You don't want to shove the poor things off to bed without any food, do you?

"I guess it *is* kind of early." Even Daniel had to chuckle.

They had fish patties and tomato scallop for supper, but only the twins were hungry. As Daniel and Katie were scraping most of their meal into the garbage, Dan said, "We oughta be putting some of this stuff in doggy bags and freezing it for next month when we may all be starving to death."

"*Not funny!*" snapped Katie.

But Mrs. Collicut managed a laugh and said, "Atta boy, Daniel."

After supper, Julie arrived, shy and contrite after her binge. Katie had to be cheerful and friendly to make sure Julie knew she hadn't been a total failure. The two girls filled out the diet charts together. Then Katie measured and weighed Julie, keeping up a running stream of chatter the whole time to cheer her up. She had to admit that this started to make her feel better too, and when she understood every single one of the math problems Julie had brought, she began to feel downright cheerful.

"Maybe I'm not such a math dummy after all," she said.

*   *   *

At last the twins were bathed, read to, in bed and fast asleep. Julie had had a diet pop in the kitchen and gone home. Katie and Daniel could hear the soft rumble of their father's snore behind the bedroom door. Hurriedly they got ready for bed themselves — teeth cleaned, ears washed, pajamas on.

Their mother was waiting for them in the living room all decked out in the blue dressing gown that their father had given her for Christmas, sitting in her favourite chair by the fireplace. It was a chilly evening and she'd lighted a fire.

"Okay, Mom," began Katie, who found that her teeth were chattering, "we're here. Shoot. Why's Dad going to the hospital?"

Mrs. Collicut took a deep breath. "He's going to the hospital because he's sick."

"You already said that. Sick with what?

What kind of disease?" Katie paused for a moment. "He's not going to *die* or anything, is he?"

"No, he's not. He's sick with something called a nervous breakdown."

"A what?"

"A nervous breakdown. It's hard to make it simple for you, but I'll take a stab at it. The doctor had to explain a lot of it even to me. It's like you're so tired that you're exhausted. All over. Every part of you. Even your head."

"I'm often exhausted," said Daniel. "But I don't have to go to the hospital."

"No. You're *not* exhausted. Not really. Or not like he is. With his kind of exhaustion, the weariness is something you can't control. He can't have a little rest and then bounce right back like you do, Dan, after you've been running a long time. The bounce is all gone out of you when you have a nervous breakdown. You have so little energy left that it becomes almost impossible to move around, or talk, or even think — or to be patient or kind. *Everything* is tired."

"Is that why he's so crabby?" asked Daniel.

Mrs. Collicut thought for a moment. "Well . . . yes and no. He's always been an impatient man and easily upset, but in the old days it was maybe something he could control if he really wanted to. Now it's much, much harder, and sometimes just not possible for him to stop being angry or sad." She picked up her knitting and started to work on it, her fingers flying at the ends of the needles.

"I still don't understand," said Katie. "Can't he just sort of *buck up*? Can't he tell himself to be nice?"

"Not right now, Katie," said Mrs. Collicut. "I've often thought exactly the same thing. But now I really don't think he can. I know this is hard to believe, but he just *can't*. He can't even *try*. He hates the way he's behaving right now, but he keeps on doing it." She paused again and bit the end of a knitting needle. "I know what it feels like," she said.

"What?"

"It's like being an elastic band that's been pulled so often it's not springy any more. It's just over-stretched and limp, like a piece of wet string. In the hospital they hope to put the elastic back into him."

"But how? How can anyone do that?" said Daniel, chewing on his fingernail. "It can't be simple, like taking out an appendix or sewing up a cut."

"No," sighed Mrs. Collicut, laying down her knitting. "It isn't one bit simple. But lots and lots of people have nervous breakdowns, and they seem to be able to work miracles for them at the hospital."

"*How*?" repeated Daniel.

"Well, to begin with, they all do a lot of talking, especially the person who's sick. They mostly talk about the things in the patient's life that make him unhappy. Your dad needs to talk about all those things."

"About Mr. Giles?"

"And about his awful job?"

"Yes," Mrs. Collicutt said. "And other things too. His mother was a very pushy lady. She scolded him all the time if he didn't win races and get prizes for being first in school. He never quite made first in his class, and then he injured his knees and couldn't run any more. So he always felt his mother was disappointed in him. He'll need to talk about things like that."

"I sure can understand how *that* feels," muttered Daniel. "Does that mean I'll be a pushy father too?"

"Well," chuckled Mrs. Collicut, "let's hope not. If you talk about it and get it out of your system, maybe you won't need to take it out on your children."

"*Complicated!*" exclaimed Katie. "And what else'll they do?" She looked out the window at the driving rain and wished that bad weather didn't always make her feel worse.

"At the hospital? Oh, they'll give him medication to relax him and let him get caught up on his sleep. Before too long, they'll ask him to join an exercise class."

"Why? He's *sick*." Katie was feeling really confused.

"Because if your head and nerves are extra

tired, it often helps a lot to exercise your body, especially to music. Even to dance. The music helps. It's beautiful and it's orderly. It's got a nice regular beat. It's soothing. And if it's quick, it can sort of perk you up."

"What else?"

Mrs. Collicut thought for a minute, fiddling with her ball of wool. Then she went on. "They give the patients tests to find out if they're happy in their work or home life, and try to help them change those things if they're all wrong. Like leaving Mr. Giles. That'll help. And maybe they'll find a way for him to do something he likes."

"For money? For paying the rent? And food?"

Mrs. Collicut got up and poked the fire. "Don't worry about that part," she said, putting another log on. "We'll have unemployment insurance benefits. And I'll get a job." She laughed. "There must be some place in Halifax that wants to hire an old lady of thirty-five who isn't trained to do anything at all!"

Katie couldn't see the funny side of this. She stared into the fire and thought about the Festival cup. She imagined it floating up the chimney on little licks of flames, like wings.

"I could stop music lessons," she forced herself to say, her voice dreary.

"We'll worry about that if it becomes necessary," said her mother.

If it becomes necessary. So it might really happen. Take away my food, my periwinkle blue sweater, my ten-year-old teddy bear, my ring that Aunt Hermia gave me — but don't take away my music! She felt as though she were closed up in a box of sadness. Right now, she couldn't see outside of it to anyone else's pain, even her father's. When she did think of him, she was ashamed to discover that she actually felt angry with him for having a nervous breakdown. How could he do this to her?

Daniel's thoughts were different from Katie's. He had a nagging fear that he might grow up and treat his own kids like his father treated him. But his mother had said this needn't happen. Maybe because of what he knew, he'd be extra kind, extra gentle with them. In a way, he was a bit relieved that his father was going into hospital. Maybe he'd come home a more peaceful person.

"Will the hospital cure him?" he asked.

"Some people say," said Mrs. Collicut, "that a nervous breakdown is the best thing that can happen to a person. It's like a second chance at life."

"A *what*?" Katie came out of her box for a moment.

"It's hard to explain," said her mother, "but it's almost as if you've broken into a hundred pieces and have a chance to glue them all tight again, only in a different, happier way. You discover things about yourself that you like, and build on that." She grinned at them. "A bit like a

Humpty Dumpty who knows how to put himself together again, because he's found out which parts of his shell are strong."

"Is it quick?" asked Daniel, eyes hopeful. "Will he be well real fast?" His eyelid was flicking, flicking.

"No," said Mrs. Collicut. "It's slow. He'll be getting treatment for a long time. But he'll often be home, and we'll have a chance to help him here, too."

"How?" Katie and Daniel asked together.

Mrs. Collicut stood up and put away her knitting. "That's something I want *you* to think about. I'll have to think about it, too. But I bet you kids can come up with some really good ideas if you try extra hard." She yawned. "Now it's time we all went to bed. After your father leaves for work tomorrow, I'm going job-hunting, so I want lots of sleep. No one will want to hire someone who has dark circles under her eyes."

As Katie climbed the stairs to bed she thought to herself, *help him*. What on earth could *I* do to help him? Still — maybe I can.

She went into the bathroom and poured herself a tub full of bubbles, then climbed in. As she soaked up the warmth she thought hard. By the time she got out, she had concocted quite a few ideas. She also wasn't feeling as sorry for herself any more.

In his room, Daniel was making a list. At the top of the page he wrote:

CURES FOR DAD

Underneath, he started to write them down: 1, 2, 3, 4, 5. He was smiling as he crawled into bed.

Chapter 8

The next day, Katie made a long entry in her diary.

Dear Diary,

Today was so chock-full that I'm scared I'll forget some of the things that happened if I don't write them down. It's nine o'clock at night already, so I guess I'll be propping my eyes open tomorrow.

I went and practised at Madame Gagnon's at seven o'clock today. I didn't mind getting up, or the walk, or the stupid Halifax rain. But I minded the music. It was so beautiful, I mean.

I'd been feeling really brave and strong, and then that new Bach piece broke me right up. When Madame Gagnon came out of her bath with a towel over her hair and no make-up and looking about a hundred years old, I was crying all over the piano keys.

I was thinking, if I have to give up music lessons, I'll just die stone cold dead. So she made me tell her the whole story. When I was through, she said something like this

(I'll try to write like she talks, with her neat French accent, but it won't be exactly the same).

"*Ma chérie*. Do not worry. I'm sad for your *papa*, but he'll be fine. Probably finer than he ever was before. But you. No, you are not fine. You are full of worry about stopping your music. Well, we will just not permit such a terrible thing."

She sat down beside me on the piano bench.

"Do you think I wish to lose my best pupil? But no. Never! So if your mother cannot find a job, I teach you anyway. Not at the conservatory. Here. I give up one bath per week and give instead to you a lesson at seven in the morning. *Pas grand-chose!*"

(That means "no big thing." I asked her.)

I said to her, "That's charity."

She said, "Charity is not such a bad word. Look it up in the *dictionnaire*. Besides, I am being charitable to myself. When you will grow up and maybe teach piano (after your big concert career!) you will understand the joy to teach a student who has a real talent. It is most pleasant. Many students, I must tell you, just go *bang, bang, bang* on the piano keys." Then she put her fingers in her ears. "It is not music that they make. It is noise."

I just read that over. It's pretty good! It

really sounds like Madame talks. If I don't end up a concert pianist or a spa director, maybe I can be a writer!

Anyway, now I have one big worry that's gone. If Mom and Dad can't afford to give me music lessons, I won't have to spend the rest of my life deteriorating. (Pretty terrific word, eh, deteriorating?)

When I got to school, I was in a real good mood. My math mark was okay again, so I gave Julie a package of sugar-free gum to thank her.

Then Olaf stopped outside the school and asked me if I had the notes for social studies homework. I'm sure I saw him taking them down himself.

But I said, "Sure thing," and sat down on the school steps and dug them out of my loose-leaf. Just then, who comes by but Rita?

She stops and puts her head on one side like a cutesy puppy and says, "Hi, Katie. Who's your *friend*?"

And then she sort of runs her fingers through her hair slowly, like they do on the TV ads for shampoo. And *bat, bat, bat* go her eyelashes. Then she wiggles off down Tower Road.

I'm just thinking, how can you be so *stupid*, Rita, when Olaf turns to me and says, kind of wide-eyed, "Who's *that*? Ever a cute girl!"

Well, all I can say is, boys sure can't see any farther than the tip of their noses. Any *girl* could see right through that silly stuff.

Pause. That was ten minutes while I crept downstairs for some pop.

When I took it out of the fridge, I thought, I bet you anything that no job means no more pop. We'll have to spend our few nickels on lettuce and healthy stuff.

I am deeply in love with junk food, but I wouldn't admit that to Julie.

Dad went to work and quit his job. When he came home at 5:30 he looked really tired, and also sad. But I think he seemed a little bit more peaceful too. Mom said later that that's because he made his decision. I asked her how she knows so much about nervous breakdowns. She said she asks the doctor a lot of questions, and also reads stuff.

I think maybe she's kind of smart, but I never thought about her like that before — being either smart or dumb. She was just my mother.

One-thirty in the morning. It looks like I fell asleep in the middle of writing. But this day was too important to forget. I'll write some more and then grab some sleep before I have to get up.

Later on in the evening, I went past the

TV room. Dad had his hand over his face and his shoulders were hunched down and sort of shaking.

I went out to the kitchen and said, "Mom. I think Dad's *crying!*"

She said, cool like, "So?"

I said, "Well, he's a *man.* And he's my *father.* I never ever saw a man cry before. Not ever."

Then she got mad. She closed the kitchen door so my dad couldn't hear, and turned the radio on. Then she stared at me with a really cross look, and said, "Well, if you never saw such a thing, it's time you did. If a man can't cry once in a while, it means he's all shut up inside and doesn't know how to let his grief get out. That's half your dad's problem. If you don't let your sadness escape once in a while, it turns inside out and gets to be something else."

I asked her, "Like what?"

She said, "Like stomach ulcers, or headaches, or a pile of terrible anger."

That doctor seems to be telling her a lot of interesting stuff.

Then she said some more. She said, "What do you expect parents to be like — the good giants in a fairy tale? Who, exactly, do you think we are? We're just people. We're just kids who have more or less grown up. But inside, we're still the same in a lot of ways.

Don't you think I ever get scared or sad? You can't expect a parent to be strong *all* the time."

I didn't know what to say. It's kind of scary to find out that parents aren't as strong as steel for ever and ever. So I didn't say anything.

Then she said, "For instance . . . "

And I said, "Yeah?"

She said, "For instance, I'm kind of nervous about my new job."

Suddenly she had her big wide smile on.

"*New job!*" I yelled. I nearly jumped on her, I was that excited.

And it turns out she has a job at the supermarket at the cash register, and she's worried she won't learn the keys fast enough.

So all of a sudden *I* felt strong. I told her computers at school aren't very hard, and I'm not even good at math. You have to learn a keyboard there too. I told her she'd be a whizz.

Then I asked her why Dad was crying.

She said, "Lots of things. No job. No pay. Sickness. Hospital in a few days. He probably can even hear his mother inside his head, saying, 'Win, win, win,' and he thinks he's lost another race."

Then she said something else that made me really think. She said, "He probably thinks he's come to the end of a road. He doesn't realize yet that he's just put his big toe onto a new one."

I felt kind of sorry for Mom, now that I knew she was only a human being like the rest of us. But in a funny way it felt good too, like she'd opened a door and let me in.

It's so late that it's early. This is the longest entry I ever put in my diary. When I'm old like my parents I'll read it and think about what a dramatic life I led when I was thirteen and a half.

Chapter 9

"Well, one thing about it," Katie said to Daniel on their way to school, "at least the twins' allergies are better. Those needles are really something. Their faces are starting to look like real live skin."

Mr. Collicut had left for the hospital the day before. His family had been so cheerful about it, you'd have thought he was going off on vacation. Mrs. Collicut had bought him a pile of mystery novels at the book exchange, and Daniel had found him a crossword puzzle book, one of the really hard ones. The twins put their money together and bought him a bag of cashews, his favourite nuts. Katie spent her whole allowance (and maybe my last one, she thought) on a beautiful hardbound book with blank pages.

"You can do anything you want with it," she told him. "You can draw pictures, or make up new crosswords, or write down all your innermost private thoughts, or make poems, or growl in it, or just keep a diary. I'd bust wide open sometimes without a diary."

Her father had laughed almost like in the old

days on the beach and said, "At this point, I'd do almost anything to keep from busting wide open."

Then they'd all driven down to the sea wall and watched the ships and the islands and the clear blue horizon and had ice cream at the canteen. They'd skipped stones on the beach and the kids had gone wading in the frigid water.

Later on, they'd all gone to Karmen's Fried Chicken for a late lunch before Mrs. Collicut drove their father to the hospital. It was like a special, festival day, except that everyone but the twins knew they were playing games with each other.

But, as Katie said that morning, things weren't all bad. At least the twins had stopped scratching. And there was something else. Their mother was half in love with her cash register and was just as big a whizz at it as Katie had predicted she would be.

On the day after her mother started her job, Katie'd gone into the supermarket by the side door after school and hidden behind the bananas and cucumbers and watched her. She couldn't believe what she saw. Already her mother's fingers were flying over the keys.

"She must be even smarter than I thought!" she said to Daniel later. "I told her it'd be easy for her to learn how to use that cash register, but I think I was secretly a little bit lying. I really thought she'd have a terrible time. I was just trying to make her feel better."

It was mid-October now, and Katie's fingers were cold as she held them up and counted.

"Three good things!" she announced. "One, I get to keep on with my piano lessons." She hummed the first three bars of a Chopin waltz as she held up her thumb. "And the twins' rashes are clearing up." She put up her index finger. "And three" — up went the middle finger — "Mum likes her job and is good at it. She doesn't make as much money as Dad did, but we're not going to starve after all."

"Four!" cried Daniel. "Yesterday I did my best time ever, and Mr. Jemseg *smiled* at me. I didn't know he *had* any smiles packed away in that gym bag of his. That man scares me half crazy."

He bit his thumb nail.

"So . . . " said Katie. "We've got four good things going for us." She looked over to the right as they approached the corner. "And here's one that's not so good."

"Hi!" called out Rita. "Wait for me!" She ran panting up to them. Her hair was freshly washed, and bounced as she walked. From time to time she reached up and patted it.

They walked along in silence for a while, and then Rita said, "Hear your dad's in the hospital."

"Yeah. Yesterday."

"Bet you're relieved, eh?"

"Whadda you mean, *relieved*? He's in the hospital, for Pete's sake!" Katie could feel a knot in her chest.

"Well, good grief, you don't need to jump on me! I just figured it'd be hard to live with someone who isn't, well, right in the head."

Daniel stopped in his tracks and grabbed Rita by the arm.

"Did you say '*not right in the head*'?"

"Well," began Rita, "You know. Like . . . not *right*. My mom says . . . "

"Exactly what does your mom say?" Katie's voice was cold and thin.

"She says — she's said for *weeks* — that anyone in that shape ought to be in a mental hospital."

"Well, he *is* in the hospital, but we don't happen to be relieved," snapped Katie. "We're sad he's gone. And what's more, we're lucky, because he'll be home every second weekend and we're all going to help him get better fast."

Rita was frowning. "Well, what's wrong with him then, if he's not crazy or anything?"

"*Crazy*!" Katie almost screamed the word.

Rita's voice was hard to hear. "Yeah, crazy. Else why is he in a mental hospital?" They had just reached the school grounds.

Katie stopped walking and faced Rita. Just below the surface of her reply, she was thinking: please just let me keep from crying while I'm talking. And keep me from bashing her face in.

92

Let me make her understand. "Because," she answered very slowly, very carefully, "if you're really exhausted — every single part of you — that's a good place to go for a while, to get strong again. My dad's nerves are really tired and worn-out right now. The hospital'll make him better. So will we. He's not *crazy*."

And then she couldn't help adding, "You dumb bunny!"

"Why, you . . . !" gasped Rita. "You don't need to call me names! I was just trying to be sympathetic!" And she flounced off toward the girls' entrance to the school.

"Sympathetic like a scorpion," muttered Katie.

"What's a scorpion?" asked Dan.

"A scorpion," said Katie, "is a small poisonous creature that sits around looking innocent and then springs at you when you're not expecting anything."

"Does it sting or bite?" asked Daniel, gnawing his nails.

"It can kill you," said Katie.

*   *   *

That afternoon, the weather was damp and dull. Daniel set off for the track field, his face tense, his feet dragging. He felt tired and he felt sad. He was doing all this track team stuff to please his father and his father wasn't even there to notice.

He had a list of things to do to help his dad get better, but he wouldn't be home for two weeks.

He was glad his mother had a job, and he was really happy that she liked it, but he missed having her at home when he got back from school. That Mrs. Flooby who came in to baby-sit was kind and made good cookies, but she just wasn't his mother. Besides, it was starting to rain, and he felt like he could use some sun today.

"Move it! Move it!" yelled Mr. Jemseg as Daniel dragged his way across the field. "There's lead in your feet, Collicut!"

"Dumb coach!" muttered Daniel under his breath, as he ran toward the group at the end of the field. Even as he raced down the track he was thinking, oh to be lying on the sofa at home reading a bunch of comics. Or finishing that really neat book I got from the school library.

Dan ran badly that afternoon. He felt as though he weighed forty-five kilograms and Mr. Jemseg was right, there *was* lead in his feet.

"Collicut!" The coach yelled to him. "Get over here where I can talk to you!"

Dan ran over to the goal posts. Other boys hung around to listen.

"Okay, Dan! Are we gonna win that pennant from Westmount School or not?"

"Yeah," said Daniel. "Sure thing."

"Not a chance," growled Mr. Jemseg. "Not if you go on running like a ninety-year-old fat lady carrying four bags of groceries. What's got into you?"

"Nuthin' much," mumbled Daniel, digging his heels into the sod.

"Nothing, my foot!" said the coach. "Out with it!"

"My dad's in the hospital," said Daniel, staring at the ground. "He went yesterday. And a bunch of other things."

"Oh!" The coach looked concerned, even *kind*. "What's the trouble?"

"A nervous breakdown," said Daniel.

There was a pause before Mr. Jemseg said anything. Then he blurted out, "A nervous breakdown! Just what I need!"

Just what *he* needs. Daniel stared. Mr. Jemseg was a handsome man, but right then he looked almost ugly to Dan.

The coach looked up at the sky and hit his forehead with his fist. "Just what I need right now!" he repeated, as though he was talking to himself. "A kid — a *nervous* kid — whose father's having a breakdown."

He looked at Daniel. "I can just imagine what's gonna happen to you during the pressure of competition. Oh, *brother*! I'm sorry for you and your father, kid, but I'm also sorry for our team."

Daniel felt something rising up inside him, more brand-new feelings. He felt fury in the face of Mr. Jemseg's injustice and unkindness, but a strange new kind of strength too, an icy calmness. Mr. Jemseg was a scary man, but Daniel felt no fear of him at all as he spoke.

"Listen, Mr. Jemseg," he said. "It took my dad thirty-four whole years to get sick from all the troubles he had. It's not gonna happen to me before the spring track meet. If you wanta put me off the team, you go right ahead and do it. That'll suit me just fine. But I happen to know that you need me on this team. And if you keep me on, you're gonna be sorry you said what you just said."

Mr. Jemseg's eyes sort of slid from side to side and he didn't answer Daniel.

He just blew his whistle and yelled, "Okay, team! Two more laps before we call it a day! Get moving!"

Daniel finished those two laps faster than he'd ever done before. Then he picked up his gear and left the field without a word to anyone.

"Well, I'll be darned!" muttered Mr. Jemseg, scratching his head.

* * *

With Mrs. Collicut working and Mr. Collicut away, there were more chores for the children. The twins folded all the laundry and cleared the table after meals. Dan looked after the garbage, dried the supper dishes, and vacuumed the living room once a week. Katie washed the dishes, took the twins for their allergy shots, was in charge of keeping the bathroom clean, and did her own mending.

"What do *you* do around here, Mom?" grumbled Ben one day.

Mrs. Collicut laughed. "I just sit around and improve the scenery," she said. Then she sobered up. "I do a lot," she said. "I bring home the bacon —"

"The *what*?" interrupted Carl.

"She means she brings home the pay cheque," explained Katie, "to *buy* the bacon. Or whatever."

"*And*," continued their mother, "I visit your dad three times a week, buy all the groceries, cook all the meals, and do stuff like writing letters and paying bills and shopping for your clothes. And mowing the lawn. I also listen to all your tales of woe and apply Band-Aids." Then she added, "On a really slow day I sometimes get to watch the eleven o'clock news. If I can stay awake that long."

That Sunday, Daniel brought his mother breakfast in bed before he went out to run. He wakened her from a sound sleep to do it.

Chapter 10

"Katie," Daniel began as they walked along toward school. There had been a big wind the night before, and the trees were almost bare. They were kicking their way through the fallen leaves, enjoying the old familiar crackle and swish.

"Dad comes home tomorrow. Did you think of any ways to help him get well? I've got a list of things to do. I can hardly wait to start curing him."

"I've got a list too," said Katie, "but mine's short. What's on yours?"

"You go first."

"Okay. Three things," she said. "Don't practise scales on the day he's home. Write him a letter for sure every week. And here's the special one. Teach him how to play the piano, and make sure he feels like he's doing good at it. Mom says this winning and losing thing is part of his problem. So I've gotta make him feel like he's a big success as a piano player."

Daniel grinned. "Great stuff!" he said. "Almost as good as mine."

"Which is?"

"I've got five things. Take out the garbage even when he's home. Don't crab if he's watching things we don't like on TV. We've got no time to watch TV any more anyway! Think up things for Ben and Carl to do when they make too much racket. Tell him how often I practise my running. And — best of all — take him running with me on the days he's home."

"What!? But he hasn't run since he hurt his knees."

"Yeah, I know. But I bet that's because he didn't want to run because he couldn't be the best in the world. His knees must've mended years and years ago."

Katie ran up the Gilligan's steps and jumped down into a giant pile of coloured leaves underneath their maple tree.

"But he's *sick*," she called out from somewhere in the middle of the heap.

"Sure. I know. But Mom says it helps your nerves to exercise. The doctor told her. So . . . "

"So won't it just bring back bad memories? 'Cause he'll be real slow at first." Katie frowned.

"Maybe you're right. It could be tricky. But I think I know something really great that he doesn't know. I'd like to show it to him, or teach it to him, or something."

"Which is?"

"I guess it's really a bunch of things, but they're all mixed up into one another. The first is that if you're gonna really knock yourself half dead working for something, it oughta be something you *like* a lot. Like acting, for me."

"Maybe he knows that by now. He knows what he *doesn't* like. He doesn't like doing three people's work for Mr. Giles."

"But he doesn't know what he *does* like," insisted Daniel. "Or *maybe* he doesn't. Anyway, he really doesn't know it when it comes to his kids."

"How d'you mean?" They'd reached the school, but they both sat down in a huge pile of leaves and went on talking.

"I mean, he still thinks *we* should do what *he* wants."

"Like?"

"Like me doing track and field so I can win medals and get to be a famous runner. Just because that's what *he* wanted for *him*."

"Well, for Pete's sake, Dan!" Katie sighed. "I don't get it. It's too late for him to win any medals now. He's *old*."

"I don't want him winning medals. That's the point. I want him to find out that running can be a fun thing when there aren't any competitions. When I started, I didn't even *like* running. Now I do — when I'm doing it where and when I want. If Mr. Jemseg fired me from the team, I'd still run in the mornings. It's real pretty at that time of day. And besides, it makes me feel strong and fast, like a horse or a cheetah or something."

"You said it's a bunch of things all mixed up

together that you want to show him. What's another thing?"

Dan hit the side of his head with his hand. "Dummy! It's all there in the one thing. After I get him back running because exercise is good for his nerves, maybe, just maybe, he'll find a thing can be fun even if you're not winning. We're doing opposite things, but maybe not."

"How do you mean, opposite?"

"I mean, you're gonna to make him feel good at his music lessons. You're gonna make him feel like a winner."

"And you?"

"I'm gonna try to make him see that winning isn't the most important thing in the world."

"Or," said Katie, "that there's more than one way of winning."

"Right!" cried Daniel, and he laughed. "Whew! I sure got tangled up trying to explain all that. I guess that's what I was trying to say all the time."

*   *   *

The next day was Saturday, and their mother went over to the hospital to pick up Mr. Collicut at two in the afternoon. He was going to be home until Sunday evening.

As soon as Mrs. Collicut came in the back door and put the keys on their hook, Katie could see by her face that the weekend wasn't going to be all that perfect.

101

When her father came in the kitchen, he smiled at them all and said, "Hi, troops! It's great to be home."

But his eyes were sad and he moved slowly, like an old man.

When he went into the TV room and sat in his old chair, he let out a sigh so long and terrible that it sounded as though nothing in the world was ever going to make him happy again.

"What's it like?" asked Daniel, coming into the room and plunking himself down on the footstool.

"What's what like?" asked his father.

"The hospital. What goes on? Is it fun at all?"

"Fun?" Mr. Collicut gave a sad laugh. "No, I wouldn't call it *fun*."

"Well, what then?"

"Oh, I don't know. We eat and sometimes we have exercises. People come and talk to me. That's good for me, I guess, but hard."

"Why hard? Just *talking*?"

"Well, they want us to talk about the tough things in our lives."

"Like Mr. Giles?"

"Yes. And other stuff. And sometimes it's very difficult to do that. But good, probably."

"Why *good*, if it's so hard?" Daniel scratched his mop of dark hair.

"Because then you get some of that really bad stuff out of you. Like poison out of an infected cut."

Katie came in and sat down on the floor beside his chair. Her face was lit up and excited.

"Dad!" she announced. "I'm gonna teach you how to play the piano! When can we start? I know you can do it. You're so musical."

Mr. Collicut passed his hand over his eyes, over his face.

"Katie," he said, his voice shaky, "thanks. But no. It's too late. I'm too old. Teach your own children when you have them."

"But *Dad*," insisted Katie, "Lotsa old people take —"

"No!" said her father sharply. He rose from the chair with an effort. "Look," he said, "I'm very tired. I think I'll go up and have a little nap. You kids go out and play or something. I'll see you at supper."

The back door opened and the twins roared through, shrieking, "Dad! Where's Dad? Is he home yet?"

When they saw him, they attacked him with hugs and he reached down and put his arms around them. There were tears in his eyes.

"C'mon, kids!" cried Daniel when the hugs were over. "I'm on my way to the library. Wanta come and get some new books?" He herded them out into the kitchen. "Remember," he whispered to them, "he's still sick. We'll see him at supper-time, after his rest."

The twins rushed off to get their library books, and then they set off.

Mrs. Collicut went upstairs with her husband, and Katie could hear the quiet murmur of her mother's voice. She sat on the floor and waited, her throat aching with the need to cry. When Mrs. Collicut came down, she got up and buried her face in her mother's chest and cried like a six year old.

"I was looking forward to it all week," she choked out. "I figured I could cure him."

They both sat down on the couch and looked at one another. Mrs. Collicut was smiling, but her voice was uneven as she spoke to Katie.

"Maybe you still can," she said. "It's really a great idea. And I agree — he's not too old to learn to play the piano. But I guess it's just too soon. He's still pretty sick." She looked off into space. "I never saw such . . . *weariness*. It must be awful!"

* * *

The rest of the weekend went on in much the same way.

Mr. Collicut responded to their presence with a kind of sorrowing affection, or with tiredness, or with irritation.

When he left for the hospital at seven o'clock the next day, Katie and Daniel lay down on the floor on their stomachs and watched TV. But they weren't really watching. There were too many other pictures inside their heads.

"He's gone," said Katie. "And Rita's right. It's a relief."

"D'you know what I think?" asked Dan.

"What?"

"I think he seems *worse*."

"Or maybe we'd just forgotten what it was like."

"Yeah, maybe."

"But anyway," sighed Katie, "I sure hope the hospital hurries up and makes him better."

They heard the car as it crunched up the alleyway, and turned their heads as their mother came into the TV room. She walked over and switched off the set. Then she sank into the sofa.

"Listen, kids," she said. "I'm sorry. I should've prepared you. The doctor told me, but I guess I tried not to believe him."

"Told you what?"

Mrs. Collicut rubbed her forehead with the tips of her fingers.

"That the first visit home is really hard. That it's a terrible strain for everyone."

She laughed a little. "He was so right!"

"Mom!" Daniel was chewing on his thumb nail. "I wanted to take him running. Is he going to be tired for ever and ever?"

"No," she said, "he isn't. And the running idea is a good one. But this is a slow business. Getting better — *all* better — could take as long as a year. And remember one thing."

"Yeah?"

"It's tough on us, but it's twenty times harder

for him. Try to keep that in mind. We have to be really patient."

As Mrs. Collicut went upstairs to put the twins to bed, Katie said to Daniel, "I'm not sure I *have* that much patience."

* * *

When the twins had had their baths and were settled under the covers, Mrs. Collicut sat down on a chair between their beds and asked, "How's it going? You guys okay?"

"No," said Carl. "It wasn't any fun. The weekend, I mean."

"No," agreed Ben. "Why isn't he all better? Why is he still so tired and grumpy?"

Mrs. Collicut sighed, and then kissed them both on the tips of their noses. "Because he's still sick. It's going to take him a long time to feel completely well again." She grinned at them. "We're all just going to have to learn to be extra good at waiting. Sometimes," she added, "that's one of the hardest things to do."

Outside, the wind was driving against the big oak tree and they could hear rain starting to beat down on the old porch roof.

Chapter 11

The next few weeks passed quickly for Katie and Daniel. Katie already knew her Festival piece by heart, and was now adding expression and grace to the bare notes of the composition. She loved that part of learning a piece: deciding how loud *forte* really meant; working on shadings of soft and hard; deciding how to put sadness or pep into the melody; knowing exactly when to speed up and slow down, and why. She had already polished her recital piece in this way. She felt she'd done all she could with it, and that it was ready.

On the night of the recital, early in November, Katie looked nervously out over the audience — and found herself looking into her father's eyes. It wasn't even his weekend to be home, and he looked pale and shy. Knowing he had made a special effort to be there gave Katie an extra burst of pride and confidence and she played well.

Afterwards, everyone congratulated her and said, "Well, *you're* certainly going to win the Festival cup this year," but her dad was nowhere in sight.

He'd gone out to the car to wait for them,

saying he was tired. But when the family joined him, his eyes were shining with an enthusiasm Katie hadn't seen for a long time.

"Oh, Katie," he said, "I wish I could do that!"

Katie didn't say anything, but she gave him a long hard look that meant, "You can. *Try*! Just ask me and I'll help you."

* * *

Daniel's life was so full that he hardly had time to worry any more. He never played ball on the vacant lot, and he only saw friends if they happened to be on the track team or in the play.

His desire to prove the coach wrong in his predictions was fierce, and he ran with a kind of savage swiftness that amazed even himself.

The rehearsals for the play were also going well. After he memorized his lines for each scene, he took pleasure, like Katie, in putting expression into them. He became funnier and funnier in his part. Sometimes even the director would start laughing, right in the middle of giving instructions to the other players.

One day he said to Dan, "You're a natural born comic. I don't suggest to many students that they take up acting professionally, because an actor's life isn't easy. There's a lot of competition for the best parts, and you may be poor all your life, but I'd sure like to see you give it a try."

Daniel's chest felt full and warm. In his head he could see his life stretching out ahead of him

— years and years of making people laugh. He liked what he saw.

He thought, how can I be so lucky to be able to do this?

His mother noticed that he'd stopped biting his nails, but she didn't mention it.

*   *   *

The twins trooped off with Katie each week for their allergy shots, and, as Daniel put it, now you could see the skin between the bumps. They spent a lot of time in the bathroom inspecting themselves in the mirror above the sink. They missed their father, but twins always have one another, so they're almost never lonely. They drew a lot, watched TV, and played imaginary games. They hunted for bears, played house, fought boxing matches, and travelled in Africa with lions and tigers.

But maybe the twins were more troubled than they seemed.

One day, Mrs. Collicut found them in her bedroom. Carl was lying in her bed with the covers pulled up to his chin. Ben had her good white linen jacket on and was listening to Carl's chest with a stethoscope made out of a length of cord and a cookie cutter. Mrs. Collicut stopped in the doorway and watched.

"Oh, my! Oh, my!" Carl was saying. "I'm very sick. Cure me fast, Dr. Smith."

Ben stood up and frowned. "Your heart is

beating fine, Mr. Collicut," he said, "but I can hear your nerves jumping around inside your stomach."

"Oh, dear! Oh, dear!" said Carl. "I want to be home with my poor children. They're so tired of waiting."

Ben patted Carl on the head. "Don't you worry one bit, Mr. Collicut. This is a good hospital and it'll make you good as new."

Carl groaned out loud. He brought his arms out from under the covers, and held his head with both hands.

"But why does it take so long? Why do I still have these awful headaches?"

"There, there," muttered Ben. "Be patient for one more week."

Mrs. Collicut came in and sat on the edge of the bed.

"Listen, kids," she said. "Ben's right. It *is* a good hospital, and I can see already that your dad's a lot better. But it won't be just one more week. It'll be a whole lot longer than that. Even a broken leg doesn't get all better in a week. I guess I didn't explain that well enough. It could be months and months. Being patient is really hard, especially if you're six years old. But that's what we're all going to have to be."

She paused. "I know what'll make you feel better!" she said, grinning.

"What?" the twins asked in unison.

"Try to think up something special to do to

110

please him the next time he comes home. I bet you can think up something really terrific. Not anything too wild and noisy. But interesting."

Carl leapt out of bed. "C'mon, Ben!" he yelled. "I've gotta neat idea. C'mon in our room and shut the door so it'll be a secret from Mom, too."

Behind that bedroom door, they planned and worked all weekend. All on their own, they made up a puppet show, a special present for their father on his next trip home. Then they asked Daniel if he'd help them with some of the details.

"Sure thing!" said Daniel. "Will I ever!" My gosh, he thought, first an actor and now a director.

*   *   *

In the meantime, Mrs. Collicut was enjoying her job more and more. She looked upon that cash register almost as a friend. It made her feel skilled and efficient, and it obeyed all her commands.

Sometimes, she mused, smiling to herself, it's better than people. You can't push people around and treat them the way I treat that cash register.

She even started thinking about computers.

One day she said to Katie, "Tell me about computers. What do they do? How do they work?"

Katie didn't know a lot about computers, but she told her mother all she could. Then on Mrs.

Collicut's next day off, she showed her around the school computer room and gave a little demonstration. Mrs. Collicut's eyes gleamed.

"Now I know what I want to do! As soon as your father's back home and well, I'm going to start taking evening courses in computers. It's a whole new world, almost magic."

She was standing in the middle of the room, hands clasped together, gazing at the machines as though she were seeing a vision.

"Gee, Mom," said Katie, squeezing her mother's hand, "you're so great. You never seem to get gloomy or crabby. Not often, anyway. How come? What's your secret recipe?"

Her mother laughed out loud, ignoring a QUIET PLEASE sign hanging from the ceiling.

"Well," she said, "I don't know. But a sense of humour sure comes in handy."

But Mrs. Collicut was very quiet on the way home. Katie's question kept repeating itself in her head. It was true that her sense of humour had taken her a long way, but only she knew how gloomy and crabby she often felt inside. It seemed to her that the whole family might collapse if she gave in to those feelings, so she hung on tight and kept smiling.

Still, she never really forgot her own doubts and fears. Should she have looked for a job earlier, taken some of the money pressures off her husband? But the twins and Mr. Collicut had both seemed to need her at home. Besides, she had so little training that it never occurred to her that anyone would want to hire her.

Then she thought, what if I'd just crossed my fingers and encouraged him to leave Mr. Giles before he became so sick that he *had* to?

But then, she reminded herself, every time we started to talk about it, he'd just end up stamping around and refusing to discuss it. Jobs are scarce in Halifax. He doesn't have that much training or education himself. To move six people to a larger centre — like Toronto, for instance — would have been too big a gamble, and an expensive one.

Mrs. Collicut took a long breath and let it out very slowly. I'm tired of propping everyone else up, she thought to herself. I really wish there was someone *I* could lean on at times. Everyone else in this family can howl with pain. I'd like to do some of that myself.

But at least things are starting to look a little brighter. Mr. Giles is no longer part of our lives and Frank is starting to get good treatment for his illness.

And then Mrs. Collicut found herself smiling. *Her job. Her cash register. Those computers.* That world had been out there all along, waiting for her to find it. And she hadn't even known about it. No wonder the knot in the pit of her stomach was starting, ever so little, to untie itself. No wonder she was beginning to feel relaxed enough to feel sorry for herself.

*   *   *

The first six weeks of Mr. Collicut's illness were the longest that Katie could ever remember.

One evening she wrote in her diary:

Dear Diary:

This nervous breakdown thing is like a teeter-totter. Every time Dad is up, we all go up with him. When he's down, do we ever hit the ground hard.

The second time he was home, he seemed almost as good as new. The next week, he was so grumpy and tired that it was like the hospital wasn't helping him at all. He got mad at Mom right in front of the whole family — just because one of his socks was missing in the dryer. He threw the one sock right across the room and knocked over an open bottle of Mom's nail polish.

Dear Diary, have you ever tried to wipe red nail polish off a white tile? Dad said it was Mom's fault for leaving it open — and stomped out of the room and slammed the kitchen door. And when Mom thought all of us were gone, I saw her pick up the same sock and throw it at the wall so hard that you'd think she wanted to *kill* it.

Then, on Dad's last visit, he was nice as pie. And calm like the harbour on a still morning. Best of all, I argued with him about something and he didn't come down on me like he used to when I didn't think the exact same thing he was thinking.

When I wake up on the morning of one of his visits home, my stomach feels like it has a big rock inside it. You just never know how it'll all go this time. And the twins are like firecrackers ready to go off. I think they feel it too. Not knowing how he'll be, I mean.

* * *

One Sunday at home, Mr. Collicut asked Daniel how his running was coming along.

"Great, Dad! My time is really fast now."

"Chip off the old block!" exclaimed his father. "Boy! If you win that regional trophy, you can go right on to the provincials. You must be dying to win."

There was a pause, then Daniel spoke: "Only because I have to prove I'm good to the coach. And to you." Dan hesitated again, then took a deep breath, bit his brand new nail, and said, "But I don't really care if we win."

"*What*? Are you *serious*?"

"Yes."

"But that's what keeps you running well. That's what makes it worthwhile. That's what makes you special."

"What does?"

"Winning."

"Dad?"

"Yes?"

"Listen. I know you don't agree. So please don't get mad. But things don't work that way for me. I hate competitions. But I love running. In the morning when it's misty and the sun is coming up and I'm tearing along by the Public Gardens, I feel like I'm flying. I feel so strong and fast and free. I feel like I could run to China."

His father looked at him strangely. "If there were no track meets, would you still run in the mornings?"

"Yes. I'll always run now. And maybe . . . "

"Maybe?"

"Maybe some morning in the spring when it's warmer and you're feeling peppy again, maybe you'll come out and run with me. I'd like that a lot."

A shadow passed over his father's face. "I dunno, son. Even the thought of running makes me sad. And kind of frantic. I'm not sure I could handle it."

Daniel knew he shouldn't press his father too hard yet. So he just said, "Well, think about it sometime. It could maybe make you happy again. Who knows?"

But his father didn't answer. He was looking out the window as though he were seeing a lot of sad things that he'd never be free of.

But you *will* be free of them, thought Daniel savagely. In the spring we'll go running together, and we'll chase all those things away.

That evening, the twins put on their puppet

show. They did it well, and Daniel helped them behind the little theatre, adding voices, changing scenes. Their father smiled and clapped and thanked them, and the twins were excited and pleased. But Daniel looked at his father and saw the deep sorrow behind his eyes again, and thought, when will it ever go away? Maybe I won't be able to help him after all.

*   *   *

Three weeks before Christmas, Mr. Collicut came home for the weekend. The supper hour was cheerful, and nobody got mad, no one seemed sad.

Suddenly Mr. Collicut said to Katie, "Play for me for a while, will you? Some jiggedy tunes. And then maybe something soft and peaceful."

Katie played. She started with some quick dance melodies and finished with a couple of Schumann pieces that were gentle and quiet. When she stopped, there was a pause. Then her father clapped and clapped.

"Katie," he said thoughtfully, "I've missed your music. And listen, there's a piano at the hospital. Once you said you'd teach me to play, and I landed on you like a tonne of bricks. Well . . . "

"Well?"

"I told the therapist about that last week. She said if I don't take you up on it, I'm crazy."

"Crazy!" Katie laughed. "Well, we don't want *that*!" she said. "When do we start?"

"You say when."

"Now." Katie felt like dancing and singing. "We've got today and Sunday. If we do a little bit tonight, and then in the morning and afternoon — just a little bit — I can teach you enough so you can practise on the hospital piano."

And they did just that. Mr. Collicut was intelligent as well as musical, and he liked to win. In this case, he wanted to win over the silent piano, over his stumbling fingers. He wanted to show the piano who was boss.

As Katie explained and demonstrated, as she showed him the notes and taught him how to read them, she could feel a power and steadiness in her father that she hadn't noticed in a long time.

"Look," said Katie just before he left on Sunday, "here's one of my first-year books. You know enough already to be able to play these pieces if you work hard. Just play the right hand for a while. If it's not too hard, you might want to try the left hand, too. By March, maybe you'll be able to play a whole piece. I'll help you every time you come home."

"Katie," said Mr. Collicut, "I can hardly wait till ten o'clock tomorrow morning."

"What's at ten o'clock tomorrow morning?"

"At ten o'clock the music room's free. The piano will be sitting there all ready for me."

That night Katie wrote in her diary:

Dear Diary:

My dad is getting better. I can feel it in

my bones. It's like we're on the beach again, playing in the sand, and I'm helping him learn how to make sand castles.

I'm tired. Goodnight.

Katie

Chapter 12

In December, Katie made a number of entries in her diary.

December 1

Dear Diary:

I'm so busy these days that I'm not going to try to write beautiful entries any more. It takes too long. But I have to remember what's going on in my life, for my old age. So I'm going to write *something*.

Today was my music lesson. Madame Gagnon told me my Festival piece is so good that she couldn't have done much better herself way back when she used to play. She also told me her aunt had a nervous breakdown when she was forty and was one hundred percent A-okay in a year. Madame gave me some tricky new exercises for making my fingers faster and more controlled.

Olaf smiled at me today in the hall, and when I smiled back I thought real hard, *graduation dance, graduation dance.* I hoped the thought waves would hit him. I'm going to do that every time I see him until

May. Then one day when he sees me, he may think, *graduation dance*! I'd better ask Katie if she wants to go with me.

I wish I was as pretty as Rita.

*　　*　　*

December 4

Dear Diary:

Dad was home all weekend. He seems a lot better. I asked him how he was doing and he said he was starting to find out who he is. I wonder what that means. *I* know who *I* am.

I told him that and he said, "Maybe you do. Maybe you're lucky that way. Me, I'm just getting to know myself. It's like I had no time before. Or maybe I was too upset or angry to take a good hard look."

I didn't know what to say because I still couldn't understand what he meant, and I'm not used to Dad talking to me about himself. He never did that before he went to the hospital.

So I said, "What's it like? Getting to know yourself, I mean."

He said, "Sometimes good and sometimes bad. It's hard to explain. In some ways I'm really getting to like myself. But I see bad things too, and I have to work on changing those things."

Pretty strange, eh, dear diary?

We worked on his piano lesson and then he went back to the hospital.

*   *   *

December 5

Dear Diary,

Dad is coming home for good on the 13th. *Friday the 13th.*

I said, "Good grief, choose another day."

But he said, "No, sirree. If they say I can come home that day, I'm not going to wait till the 14th."

Daniel's play is on the 14th. I hope it doesn't shock Dad so much that he has to go back to the hospital. Mom says it won't. She checked with the doctor. But it worries me.

It doesn't worry Daniel. Nothing seems to worry him these days. Has he ever changed. Maybe, like Dad, he's getting to know himself too.

I really do think that I know who I am. I wonder if that's possible.

*   *   *

December 8

Dear Diary,

Julie was over tonight to get weighed in. She's lost six kilograms. Her pretty face is peeking out from behind all that fat. You'd think I'd given her a million dollars. She's changed inside too. She's not so shy, and she smiles a lot.

Her shape is changing much faster than my math, but I'm doing okay. I'm pretty certain I'll pass. But I sure am dumb at it. When it gets me down, I go play the piano. That fixes me right up. Someone once told me that music is mathematical. Did you ever hear such a dumb idea?

*   *   *

On the 13th, Mr. Collicut arrived home at noon. It was a crisp sunny day with new fallen snow on the ground. Mrs. Collicut picked him up during her lunch hour, then left him to unpack and rest up while she went back to work.

The first thing Mr. Collicut did was take a nap. Then he got up and went for a short walk. The snow on the trees made him feel peaceful inside, and there was something hopeful in the crisp air. Best of all was the thought that he would be returning to his own house when the walk was over.

When he arrived there, Daniel was inside waiting for him.

"Welcome home, Dad!" he said, and hugged him hard. "Want a cuppa instant coffee? Tea? Or what?"

"How about tea?" said Mr. Collicut. "That'd be nice."

When Daniel brought the tea, he sat down in the kitchen beside his father.

"No track practice today," he said. "Mr. Jemseg had to go to a workshop or something. To teach coaches how to coach. Me, I think he could learn a few things about that himself."

"Like what?"

"Like maybe that you can be a good coach without growling at the kids all the time."

"Maybe," said his father. "I hope so."

"Dad?"

"Yes?"

"I have something to confess. Maybe you'll be real mad, but I have to tell you anyway."

"Shoot, son. I'll try to keep my cool. I'm getting kind of good at it. Sometimes, anyway."

"Okay, Dad." Daniel was finding it wasn't as easy as he'd expected. "You know that play I tried out for?"

"Yes."

"Well, when the director called up to say I had been chosen for the part, I promised I'd take it. I *promised*. You shouldn't break promises, right?"

"Well . . . "

"And besides, I wanted to do it so badly, I was almost crazy. I was scared that if I broke my promise he'd never trust me again. Never give me another part. Dad?"

"Yes?"

"I knew it was what I wanted. So . . . "

"So?"

"So I disobeyed you. I took the part."

Daniel waited. Mr. Collicut just sat there, looking at him as though he were thinking. He kept making little circles on the kitchen table with his index finger. Dan wondered if he was ever going to speak. Finally, his father broke the silence. "I can see it was a tough decision, Dan," he said. "I would've hit the roof back then if I'd known, and to tell you the truth, I came pretty close to hitting the roof just now. But I can see a lot of things clearer now. You shouldn't have broken your promise, and you shouldn't have disobeyed me. You were really up a tree. How did you fit it all in? How did the school work go?"

"Fine. My marks are fine. I worked really hard. You were right. It *is* too hard doing all that. But I figured I could survive it for just one year without dropping dead in my tracks. But I had to give up a lot of stuff. Like friends. That was hard."

"And the track? It was your first commitment, you know."

"Fine, too. You'll see. The meet is in May."

Mr. Collicut took a long breath and let it out slowly. "Next time," he said, "let's discuss it first." He laughed, and reached out to rumple Daniel's hair. "I'm better at discussing, now. Not always. But usually. I find it a lot more productive than yelling at everybody, and less tiring."

"Whaddaya mean, productive?"

"Oh, you know. Better things come out of it. But anyway, I'm glad it all worked out okay for you. How's the play?"

Daniel jumped up, eyes shining. "Terrific!" he exclaimed. "I love it! And I know it's really what I want to do most of all. Forever!"

"If it really is," said his father, "and you know that already, you're lucky. You may change your mind six or seven times before you grow up. But then again, maybe you won't." He paused and looked hard at Dan. "I'm thirty-three years old, and I've just found out what I want."

"Hey, wow, Dad!" Daniel leapt right off the floor this time. "What is it? How'd you find out? It sure isn't Mr. Giles!"

Mr. Collicut chuckled. "No, it isn't. It's carpentry. We had all kinds of things to try at the hospital, and lots of tests — aptitude tests, they're called — to find out what's really right for the patients. It seemed to take forever for me to find exactly the right thing, although the tests did show that I liked working with my hands. Then . . . "

"What? Then what?"

"Three weeks ago, a man started coming to teach carpentry. It was so great to take a bunch of wood and some nails and screws and stuff, a pile of nothing, really, and make them into real things, sometimes beautiful things — tables, bookcases, all sorts of furniture, and for some people, whole houses. Suddenly it was like one of

126

those kids' toys where you try to put pegs in different holes. All the pegs started falling into the right places."

"I know!" Daniel almost yelled. "I know *exactly* how you felt. It was like that the very first time I was in a play at cub camp. Everything was suddenly . . . *right*!"

"Aren't we lucky!" grinned his father. "You and me."

Just then, Katie came in the back door with the twins, fresh from the allergist. They all roared into the kitchen without even taking off their coats and piled onto their father, welcoming him home.

"Listen! Hey, kids, listen!" Daniel shouted above the racket. "Dad wants to be a carpenter."

"Ever *neat*!" breathed Katie. "You'll be able to make all kinds of things — desks, stools, cupboards, even buildings!"

"D'ya know how?" asked Ben.

"Stupid!" scoffed Carl. "Of course he knows how!"

"No," said their father. "I *don't* know how. But I want very hard to know how. As hard as Dan wants to know about acting and Katie wants to know about music and your mother wants to know about computers." He stopped and looked at Ben and Carl. "What do you guys want very hard?"

Ben spoke for both of them. "We both want

the same thing. We want to hunt lions and tigers in Africa."

"Well," laughed Mr. Collicut, "that means we all know what we want. In January I'm going to start to learn how to be a carpenter at the Halifax Vocational School. It looks like next term we'll *all* be doing homework."

*   *   *

The next night, the houselights dimmed in the school auditorium at eight sharp and a murmur of expectation moved through the audience as the curtain rose.

On the floor in the centre of the darkened stage sat a clown slumped over, his painted smiling face resting on one hand. With his free hand he occasionally wiped away a tear as he sighed.

The audience settled into hushed attention. Suddenly a young boy with an exaggerated down-turned mouth burst out of the wings and dashed towards centre stage.

"Dad! Hey, Dad!" he yelled.

As the clown slowly turned to watch him, the racing figure fell flat on his face, not in a relaxed heap, but with a smashing thud.

For a moment there was no sound. The audience sat in shocked silence, fearful that this awful fall had been unintentional. But when the clown's son — Daniel — sat up and rubbed the side of his face, sitting in a position identical to

128

his father's, they knew it was okay. Their laughter was relieved and instant.

Daniel kept them laughing through the whole play. The part of the clown's son included many falls and much clumsiness, and Daniel carried the moves off to perfection.

It was his perfect control of his body, his athleticism, that made him so good. He tripped over things; stood teetering back and forth on his heels; managed to look as though his limbs had been attached to his body with cooked spaghetti; tumbled into scenery.

And always, his well-rehearsed moves seemed natural and spontaneous. Everything he did on stage was done with such ease and confidence that he made the audience relax, too. He made them *want* to laugh. He never overacted. His body movements and his facial expressions, even through his painted clown face, were just right to let the audience know what he was thinking and feeling. He stole the show.

Even when he did all the wrong things — laughed when the scene was sad, cried when everyone else was laughing, interrupted when any other son would have known enough to shut up — he made them look natural, too. And somehow or other, in the course of the story he managed to be the one person who brought about the happy ending, who dried up the tears of The Clown Who Cried. The audience loved him.

There were six curtain calls after the play

ended. Finally, the cast did the last short scene all over again.

When Daniel came forward alone for his last bow, he fell flat on his face as he reached centre stage. Then he stood up on his rubber legs and bowed so low that his elbows almost brushed the floor. Applause and laughter vibrated through the auditorium.

Later on, when Daniel was taking off his make-up, he experienced a mixture of satisfaction and excitement that he'd never felt before.

This year, he thought, I've felt so many things that are different that I almost think I've got a brand new head.

When he met his family afterwards, his face all scrubbed and not looking one bit like the clown's son any more, his father was the first to speak.

"I couldn't be more proud of you, Dan," he said, and hugged and kissed him, right in front of everybody.

*   *   *

Late at night on December 25th, Katie made an entry in her diary.

Dear Diary:

   I'm too sleepy to write for long, but I have to say this much.

   It was the best Christmas I ever remember. We didn't have a whole lot of presents, but it didn't matter. We were all together and it was very peaceful. Now I know what they mean by *peace on earth*. They're not just talking about guns and bombs and things. They're talking about families too.

Dad made each of us something from occupational therapy. Then after dinner, he said, "Katie, I have one special present just for you."

He told me to close my eyes until he said to open them. Then he said "Open!" and I opened.

There he was on the bench in front of the piano. He had a book of music in front of him and he was sitting up very straight, like a little kid who's just starting to learn. Then he played *Silent Night, Holy Night* right from start to finish. It was slow and kind of jerky, but he didn't make one single mistake. When he turned around to bow, he looked happy enough for his face to crack.

I could feel the tears running down my cheeks and I didn't even care who saw. After all, Mom says it's quite all right for people to cry from time to time.

Chapter 13

January was a busy month. Everyone was back in school, even Mr. Collicut. He was going to the vocational school part time because he sometimes felt too wobbly to handle a full day. He still tired easily, and he often had days when he felt sad or irritable.

Mrs. Collicut continued her work at the supermarket and learned about computers at night school.

A long piece of paper on the kitchen wall listed everyone's chores. Even Daniel could cook simple meals by the end of January, and Mr. Collicut was a whiz at omelettes and salads. Katie was almost as good a cook as her mother, but Mrs. Collicut laughed and said it wasn't very hard to be as good as *she* was.

She also said that since the Collicut Domestic Team had taken over her house, it had never been so clean.

But maybe, sighed Katie later, things were going just too smoothly. On January 29th, just one month before the Festival, she slipped on a piece of ice and fractured one of the two main bones in her forearm. The pain was so bad that she fainted right there on the sidewalk. When she woke up, she saw — actually *saw* — the Festival cup floating through the air and out the window.

"It's just a small injury," said the doctor. "It's a crack, really, not broken right through. You'll be four hundred percent better by April or May."

Katie crossed all four fingers on her good hand and prayed, "Please, please, please."

Then she said, "If it's so little, I can practise, can't I?" She grabbed the doctor's arm as she asked the question, to make him say yes. *"Please!"*

"No," he said. "I'm sorry, but you can't. You'll have to be in a cast for six weeks if you want your arm to mend properly."

Katie fled to Madame Gagnon's that evening, arm in a sling. When the door opened, she just walked in without saying a word and sat down on the sofa. Madame came over and sat down beside her.

"Ma pauvre petite amie!" breathed Madame. "How did you do such a terrible thing?"

"Ice," said Katie. "Fell. I could die."

She told the whole story and then she cried for five full minutes, blowing her nose with her left hand, sobbing, hiccupping. Madame went off to the kitchen and brought back a cold glass of cola.

"Drink that," she said. "Now, *ma chére*, I am almost as sad as you. But not quite. By now I am old and I know that there will be other Festivals. But you, you think that a year is forever. But, truly, it is not the end of the world."

"Yes, it is. *It is so!*"

"But, no," insisted Madame. "Very full of disappointment, but not the end of the world. May I please make a little advice?"

"I suppose so," Katie sighed.

"Use your practise time for the next few weeks to help your *papa* with his music."

Katie frowned. "I'm tired of helping people," she said. "Right now, I wish someone would help me."

"That's what I try to do this very instant," said Madame tartly. "You wonder why I'm a little bit stern with you when you are sad?"

"Yes. I thought you'd try to fix me up."

"*Eh bien*, I can't. Not the way you want. I'm stern because I suddenly feel the big jealousy."

"The *what?* Jealousy?"

"Yes." Madame got up from the sofa and paced up and down her small living room. "Have you ever wonder why I teach instead of play? I was very good. I have won international competitions. I was concert pianist."

"Then why . . . ?"

"*Exactement!* Why? Because when I was twenty-seven years old, I was standing one day at the piano — a *grand* piano — and the whole top slam down on my wrist. My *wrist*. Katie, do you know how many bones there are in the wrist?

Eight. Do you know what happen to the hand when the wrist bones are crushed? Crushed, I say."

Katie wasn't even breathing. "*Crushed?*" she whispered.

"Crushed. If your wrist is crushed, you maybe get better enough to play again. But not without pain, nor with excellent skill. Not on the concert stage. You are finished."

Madame said this last sentence very quietly and Katie found herself repeating it silently, her lips moving, "You are finished."

"So," Madame smiled again and took a long deep breath, "I am jealous of your little crack." She laughed a little. "It is funny, *c'est drôle*, because I never had the jealousy when you were well and playing very beautifully. Now that you are hurt, I am very jealous. Because when you are one year older — before you are even fifteen years old — you will be as good as new. This makes me suddenly very, very jealous."

"Oh, Madame," began Katie, blowing her nose again and mopping up her face, "I shouldn't have — "

"Nonsense!" said Madame sharply. "You speak the nonsense. Of course you are very, very sad, and you are right to cry till you are almost sick. Just as I am right to tell you about my own big misery. I am very sorry for you, even if I am jealous. I am not a big ogre. And I am not really unhappy with my own life, not any more. Except sometimes the sadness, it comes back to me. Like right now. But it will pass."

"But *why* aren't you unhappy? I'd go lock myself in a dark room and never come out." Katie looked hard at Madame Gagnon, sitting there in her strange dressing gown, her face lined and old — and *finished*.

She tried to imagine her as a young girl bent over the piano keys executing her trills, bringing her hands down on a final thundering chord, rising from the bench slowly, the folds of her long green dress swirling around her as she walked to the centre of the stage to take her bow.

"How can you *not* be unhappy?"

Madame Gagnon smiled again. "Because I teach. And I love to teach. Sometimes not, of course, if my pupils have no talent. But with you as pupil, it is almost as great a joy as to play. That is why I say, go teach your father — and heal yourself. And you'll help him too. And not just by teaching him music."

"I don't understand."

"Well, I'm not going to explain," said Madame Gagnon. "You'll find out."

* * *

It was a sad walk home for Katie. Her arm hurt, but that pain was nothing compared to the ache inside her heart. Even so, she was already starting to map out a schedule for her father, choosing finger exercises, thinking which pieces

136

were easy enough to teach him, deciding how much he should practise each day. By the time she reached home, her eyes weren't even red any more.

When she let herself in the back door, her father was in the kitchen alone, peeling potatoes, looking tired. Katie hung up her coat in the back porch and came in to sit down at the kitchen table.

"Sit down, Dad," she said. "Forget the potatoes for a minute. I've got a big problem. I need you. I need you to be my full-time piano pupil. *I need you*," she repeated.

Mr. Collicut sat down slowly. "You need me," he said. He said it with a kind of wonder. His eyes shone and his smile brought back the beach again, and Katie was riding over the waves on his shoulders.

"I really have appreciated all your help, Katie," he said, "but sometimes a sick person gets tired of having to be propped up all the time. You'd like to be able to do a little propping yourself. So this is the best gift you've given me yet. If being your full-time student is going to help *you*, well, you've got a full-time student. When do we start?"

Katie grinned. "After supper," she said.

Oh, you smart, smart lady, Madame, thought Katie, as she went upstairs to make up her father's first lesson plan.

Chapter 14

Spring was wet that year in Nova Scotia. On May 15th, Daniel looked out his window to a world that was grey and invisible. He had seldom seen such dense fog. If it stays like this all day, he thought, the hurdlers won't even be able to see the hurdles. The sprinters will crash into each other. Even a rainstorm would be better than this. He hauled his track clothes on and combed his hair with his fingers. As he pulled on his socks, he looked at his legs with a feeling of amazement. Can these muscles really belong to me? He tensed his calf muscle and felt it. It was hard, like granite.

Downstairs, all was quiet. He made his own breakfast and ate it, but a hard knot of tension in the middle of his stomach had taken away his appetite. The inter-school track meet was to be held at ten o'clock. He frowned. Mustn't have a full stomach. But I still need fuel to burn. He ate slowly and hoped the food wouldn't just stay in a lump inside him.

Daniel's whole family was coming to the meet, but he left early in order to take part in the warm-up exercises. He was nervous, but that was one thing the coach was not going to find out about. Not if he could help it.

At the Dalhousie track, Dan joked with his friends and warmed up in the ways they'd been taught to do.

At 9:30, the grey clouds brightened and gradually a light spot in the eastern sky grew round and brilliant. By 9:45 the sun had pierced the fog and Dan could see the hurdles, the track, the stands filling with parents and friends from all the city schools.

The whole Dalhousie Sports Complex was visible. The judges were sitting at long tables in front of the stage, shuffling papers, talking among themselves, adjusting their stopwatches.

Daniel was in three races: the all-school relay race with the school team, the 100-metre and the 800-metre.

The field in the centre of the track was covered with kids doing warm-up exercises — bending, stretching, flexing, running on the spot. Everyone could feel the tension in the air that comes before a large sports competition.

Daniel thought about his early morning runs. He thought about the dim light, the cool mists along the Northwest Arm, the flowers in the Public Gardens during the summer months, the thick trees along Spring Garden Road and Summer Street.

He wished he were there now instead of experiencing this steel fist in his chest and stomach. He could visualize his breakfast sitting inside him in a hard wet ball. He started to daydream about running in Point Pleasant Park sometime, beside the harbour mouth and in view of the open sea, and then into the woods with their giant pine trees and long, long paths. But you couldn't go there alone. He'd probably never get to go running there until he was grown up.

Then he heard Mr. Jemseg's voice yelling (*always* yelling, it seemed), "*Daniel*! Get the heck over here! D'you think this is a party, for Pete's sake?!"

When Daniel reached him, the coach said, "Good grief, kid! Can't you even keep your mind on things on the day of the *meet*? I've been calling you for five minutes!"

Good, thought Daniel. He's making me mad. I'll have all that adrenalin to work with. When I'm mad, I can run my legs right off.

Aloud he said, "Sorry, Mr. Jemseg. I didn't hear you."

"Well, keep your head screwed on when you're out there on the track. Do you want us to *lose*, or *what*?"

Keep it up, Mr. Jemseg, thought Daniel, and I'll break the sound barrier. Over in the stands he could make out his dad's red sweater and the twins' yellow heads. In between were his mother and Katie.

He waved and they waved back. So they must've been watching him. His mouth felt dry

and he wished he had a glass of water. The loud-
speaker blared for the commencement of races.

First came the girls' 400-metre. Then the
hurdles. Then the all-school relay.

Dan's team came third, after George Harris
tripped and fell in the last lap, twisting his ankle.

"Darn it!" frowned the coach. "So close! For
gosh sakes, you guys, try to stay on your feet.
George! Go over to the first aid station and see if
they can patch you up for the next race." George
limped forlornly across to the station.

Daniel gritted his teeth. Don't ask him how
he feels or anything. Don't say, "Tough luck,
kid," or "I bet it hurts." Be sure to make him feel
worse than he already does. Just keep trying, Mr.
Jemseg, and every one of us is going to feel like a
failure. Or mad enough to win.

Four races later came the 100-metre race for
the 10-12 age group. This was another one of
Dan's. He ran well, and he ran quickly.

Jeff Hennessey, that streak of lightning from
St. Thomas Aquinas, reached the finish first, and
Dan came second out of thirty-eight runners.

That's a blue ribbon, he thought. For me. For
the school. For the coach. For my father. He felt a
warm surge of happiness inside.

He could see the coach running over to him,
and Daniel grinned, anticipating Mr. Jemseg's
pleasure.

"Look, Collicut," he was yelling, frowning,
"we need a *first*. We're in second place overall,

and that's not good enough. A second is okay, but no big deal. Your next race will be coming up in about fifteen minutes. Don't make a mess of it!"

A mess of it! By the time the fifteen minutes had gone by, Daniel had enough anger in him, enough adrenalin, for six races. But this was the long one, the 800-metres. He couldn't always count on his endurance in this race, and he thought about Rita's remark during the first week she'd been in Halifax, when she'd said that with his short legs, he had to move twice as fast just to keep up.

But when the whistle blew, he ran as though he was jet-propelled. His feet went pounding along the cinders at such a speed that they didn't feel as though they belonged to him. But they were controlled. Dan's mind was clear and savagely concentrated. It stayed that way for two-thirds of his long journey.

Then suddenly he felt as though all the strength had leaked out of him, and he realized he'd poured the whole of his energy into the first part of the race. Now, when he needed it most, there seemed to be almost nothing left.

Although he'd been far ahead, two runners now passed him, one after the other. And there, looming up before him, was Mr. Jemseg, yelling, "Lead in your boots! Lead in your boots! Move those legs, Collicut!"

Daniel could feel the old anger filling his

body with strength again. Other words came into his head, feeding his fury.

" . . . all I need right now! A kid, a *nervous* kid, whose father is having a breakdown."

And just fifteen minutes ago: "A second is okay, but no big deal." And, "Don't make a mess of it!"

Suddenly Daniel seemed to get his second, his third, his fourth wind. His legs, slow and aching just a few seconds before, propelled him along the track with a speed he didn't know he possessed.

He passed one runner and then the other, reaching the finish line three seconds before the boy behind him and thereby breaking the record for that distance in his age group for the entire Maritime region.

When he jogged back along the track below the stands, he could see his whole family standing up screaming. He waved to them and grinned.

When he reached the coach, Mr. Jemseg said, "Nice going, kid," and slapped him on the back.

Well, how about that, thought Daniel.

The family walked home from the meet together.

"This sure is your year, Dan," said Katie wistfully. "Are we ever proud of you!"

On Daniel's chest was a blue ribbon for coming second and a red one for coming first.

Around his neck was a medal for breaking a speed record.

"Dan," said his father. "You know, I think you're even better than I was. What now?"

"What now?" Daniel looked at his father and thought about his answer. He hated to disappoint him now that he was feeling so much better.

He took a deep breath and began, "Dad, that's my last race. There's a bunch of other things I'd like to try. Like swimming. Or maybe gymnastics. Or I'd like to do hockey for a while. But just for fun. The thing I'll be doing most is acting. The director says he has a part in next year's play that I'm really gonna want. A funny part."

Mr. Collicut walked along in silence for a while. Then he said, "If that's what you really want, Daniel, fine. I have to admit I can't understand it, and I can't help feeling sad about it. It's not what *I'd* want, but I guess I'm going to have to try hard to remember that you're not me. You're you."

Daniel looked at his father, eyes shining. "Thanks, Dad," he said. There was no fog left now, and the noonday sun was warm, like summer.

Chapter 15

Late in May, Katie met Rita on her way home from school.

"I asked Olaf to the graduation dance," said Rita.

Katie could feel her heart skipping a beat or two.

"Oh?" she said, trying to sound casual.

"Yeah. But he said he was planning to ask someone else. That new girl from Ontario with the dark brown hair, I bet. The one with the eyelashes two centimetres long."

"Maybe so," said Katie, her heart pumping more or less normally again.

Rita looked at her. "Your dad seems all better."

"Yeah. He's great. Maybe not *all* better, but three-quarters of the way there."

"Maybe that's what my mom needs. A nervous breakdown, I mean."

"Why? It's no barrel of fun, you know."

"Well, she's awful crabby all the time. And nervous as a cat. About everything — traffic, kids, bugs, burglars, deep water, high places — like the kitchen stool, for heaven's sake — and muggings. If you even say *boo* to her she jumps a metre off the floor."

"Oh, well. She's likely just tired or something. She'll probably be okay."

"I sure hope so. Hey, Katie . . . "

"Yeah?"

"My mom knows Mrs. Giles," said Rita. "She says Mr. Giles was mad as hops when your dad quit his job. She says he had to hire two men to take his place, plus a student to work part-time. No wonder he was furious."

"Was that all he was? Furious?"

Rita puckered up her pretty eyebrows and asked, puzzled, "Whaddaya mean?"

"Think about it," said Katie. "If you can't figure that one out, I'm not gonna waste my energy explaining it. Bye now."

Katie left Rita at her walkway, and headed for home.

What new brunette from Ontario with eyelashes two centimetres long? Katie was frowning as she went in the back door.

* * *

That afternoon, Julie called for Katie on her way to school, although it was out of her way. As she came up the steps, Katie realized that if the Julie she saw now had come up those same steps seven months ago, she wouldn't have recognized her.

It wasn't just that she wasn't fat any more. It was other things. She looked glowing and healthy, less pasty-faced. She walked as though she loved moving, as though she enjoyed being herself.

Wow! thought Katie.

"Katie!" Julie's voice was almost a whisper. "Guess what! Jim Delaney asked me to the graduation dance!"

Katie gave Julie a big hug and cried, "Great stuff! Congratulations! You're on the way, kid!"

Inside, she was thinking, my health spa graduate has cashed in on all my lessons, but here I am without an invitation myself. No Festival, no dance, no medals for me this year.

"It's kind of disgusting, you know," said Julie.

"What is?"

"That I had to get thin before a boy took any notice of me."

"I agree. You were just as nice *inside* when you were fat."

"When I was fat, I always kept hoping that some boy would notice my beautiful *soul*."

"Yeah," grinned Katie. "It sure isn't fair. Like in Mrs. Kenton's class, who's gonna want to snuggle up to big old Harold Hopkins and his four chins? And I bet he's nice inside, too."

Then she laughed. "But we shouldn't be too shocked by the human race. There are even some birds that ruffle up their feathers before they do a mating dance."

*   *   *

After school, Olaf was waiting on the corner

147

when Katie turned down Inglis Street on the way to her music lesson.

"Hi," he said.

"Hi," she said. They stood facing one another. She considered batting her eyelashes, but decided against it. I'm just not the type, she thought. Besides, I'm not sure I know how to do it.

Olaf looked at his feet and then he studied the tree behind her left ear. He kicked some pebbles around in the dust, and said, "Uh . . . "

"Mmm?" asked Katie.

"Well," he mumbled, biting his lower lip, scratching the side of his leg, loosening the neck of his T-shirt, coughing a bit, "I was wondering. Probably you're going with someone else already. I feel so stupid asking. But what I was wondering was . . . "

Katie shut her eyes briefly, and then looked up at the cloudless May sky above Olaf's head.

Thank you, she said silently, to whatever power had arranged this state of affairs.

* * *

Late in June, Katie made this entry in her diary:

Dear Diary,

I'm sure I couldn't have survived this year without you, dear diary. Everyone in the family was trying so hard all year not to rock the boat that I think I would have gone up in smoke if I hadn't been able to spill all the things I was *really* feeling — on paper.

Boy, would Mrs. MacDonald ever love

that sentence. I sure would get zero if it was in a composition.

I haven't written for quite a while because so much has been happening that it seemed like I didn't have the time or the energy, or maybe the *need*.

Here are some things that have been going on. I'll do it fast, because tomorrow is graduation day and I want to go to bed and get my beauty sleep.

— I passed my Math exam.

— Hurray for Julie! She lost thirteen instead of twelve kilograms, and looks really neat. She says that's enough. She doesn't want to lose her curves. Jim Delaney told her he doesn't like girls to be too thin or too fat. He says he likes them just right. That's what she is.

— The graduation dance was perfect. Dancing is as good as playing the piano. Better in some ways. Like I can't play the piano with Olaf Hensen. He said he liked my dress, and called me Taffy all evening.

Mom made my dress. It's pale blue eyelet with a square neck, and a skirt that's at least ten kilometres around. It was a formal dance. Maybe I didn't tell you that before. I forgot about the long skirt when I went upstairs to the washroom in intermission. I started to run up two steps at a time and almost fell on my face. But no one was looking. Then I picked up my huge skirt and walked up to the second floor, slowly, slowly. I tried to pretend I was Lady Diana.

I said to myself, "I must keep my head up straight so my tiara won't fall off."

I wanted the evening to go on forever.

— Dad is so much better that I can't believe he's the same person he was last September. But he still has bad days when you can see that sad thing in his eyes, or when he seems to be too tired to move. But Mom says the doctor thinks he'll be one hundred percent A-okay by this September. In fact, probably more like a hundred and twenty-five percent. Better than ever.

That's enough writing for tonight. Next year is high school. That's pretty scary, but I guess if I can live through this past year, I can handle Queen Elizabeth High. Even the long walk up Robie Street. I hope so. Anyway, I'm not going to wreck the summer worrying about it.

* * *

On Saturday morning, Daniel got up extra early. It was the kind of morning he loved best. There was mist hanging close to the earth, but the late June sun was sending long low rays through it, making the world look golden and new. He crept downstairs quietly, so as not to waken anyone. It was only six o'clock. Not many people want to get up that early on a Saturday.

When he went into the kitchen for a glass of

juice before setting off on his morning run, his father was sitting at the kitchen table dressed in an ancient track suit.

"Never threw it away," grinned Mr. Collicut, patting the sweat shirt and the baggy pants. "Figured it was the only trophy I'd ever win."

Daniel just stood there not knowing what to say.

"Dan."

"Yeah?"

"Music isn't the only thing I've been practising."

"Oh, my gosh, Dad!"

"C'mon," said his father. "Get that juice down and let's go. I thought we'd drive down to Point Pleasant Park and run along the shore paths."

Daniel didn't say a word. He just gulped down his juice and then ran out to the car.

Down by Point Pleasant Park, they passed the Container Port and parked beside the old sea wall. Then they ran along by the harbour and out toward the open sea.

A tugboat chugged out to meet a large vessel, and a big oil tanker was making its way to the far horizon. Seagulls were wheeling in and out of the mist, their feathers a blinding silver as they flew into the sun. Ducks were riding on the smooth water of the morning sea, and the air was full of the biting smells of salt, tar and fish.

When Dan and his father left the shore paths and jogged along the forest roads, the trees towered above them. Under their feet, the ground was soft with pine needles.

Daniel kept his pace down a bit in case his father tired easily. But Mr. Collicut had obviously been doing a lot of secret running, and he was strong and firm. He didn't try to pass Dan, though. The two of them ran along together easily and comfortably, perfectly timed, in moving harmony.

When they arrived back home, Dan said, "Just a sec, Dad. Don't go in yet. I've got something to give you. Something special. I'll get it." He went in the house, and came back a few minutes later.

"Shut your eyes," he said when he returned. "And open your hands."

When Daniel placed the object in his hands, Mr. Collicut closed them without opening his eyes. He paused for a moment before he spoke.

"It's your medal, Dan," he said at last. "I know. I can feel it. Why? I don't understand."

Then he opened his eyes and looked at Daniel's face.

"It's for you," said Dan. "For winning." Then he added, "And because I love you."